Lilly: Beyond the Horizon

Rachel Trusty

CONTENTS

Part One
Hope

June

I took a quick breath of freezing air and scanned the thick woods around me. I was alone in the night, my heart pounding, with no one to turn to. We had traveled deep into the forest and stayed in tents while my father hunted. After two weeks, my mother had a baby, a tiny, frail baby. My mother and father were not pleased.

The night felt endless; the infant's wails rang through the darkened forest. Sometime after midnight, Mother refused to get up and feed her again; she said it could wait. I decided to take the little baby back to the tent I shared with my younger brother, Joshua. I wrapped her in everything I could find and sat with her on the cold ground.

I nestled a cup of water in the coals from our dinner fire. I stared at the mug while it warmed, hoping water would keep my little sister alive until morning. I dipped my finger in, and put it in the baby's mouth. She closed her little lips around the tip of my small finger, sucking off all the water. I did it again and again, trying to get as much in her as I could.

Every time she woke that night, I gave her more water. My mother finally fed her when *morning came, but that night I had to sit up with the her again.*

The next day we took our tents and hiked further into the hills. We stopped to rest in the afternoon; but Father walked on, carrying the baby. I didn't ask why. I was afraid for her to be taken away from me, even for an hour; but the only choice I had was to let her go. My mother slept while my father was gone. I worked to pass the time: doing the wash, gathering firewood and other small chores, always watching for my father's return.

He was gone for a couple of hours. When he came back through the woods he did not have the little wicker basket. My young, eight-year-old heart broke in that instant. I ran to him, pulling at his hands, begging him to tell me where the baby was. It was no use; he shoved me away without even looking at me.

We returned to our camp that night, and stayed there for three days, then went back to our home in the settlement. My mother and father never told me what he did with the infant. I only heard the story they told others. My heart was broken by the life I lived. Broken more for the life my baby sister would never live. I loved that little girl, more than I ever knew a person could love.

Lilly

Sitting atop my horse, I gazed down into the valley below. The forest stood behind me. Winding brooks found their way down the side of the mountain, into the valley, and went rambling toward a village in the distance. A few scattered, thatch-roofed cottages and a white-washed church steeple were visible from the hilltop. The setting sun glinted off each little stream, and the forest already lay deep in shadow.

I turned my white mare around, galloped across a stretch of grass, and reentered the narrow, wooded path. After several minutes' ride, I came to a clearing in the woods with a small cottage at its center. It had deteriorating thatch, and sagging walls. It was the only home I'd ever known.

As I neared the house, I saw Aunt Matilda sitting in her rocking chair knitting, her blind eyes raised to the surrounding forest.

I pulled my horse, Shandra, to a stop, jumped down, and tied her rope to the hitching post. Aunt Matilda smiled but continued her work as I approached the stone patio, "Did you enjoy your ride?"

I sat down beside her chair, "Yes, it's a

beautiful night."

"That it is," she replied softly, her wrinkled hands working swiftly.

The sun had sunk beyond view. The forest was still as crickets began to chirp. As I sat listening, my mind wandered to the little village in the valley below. I knew that families lived in those cottages. Aunt Matilda had told me stories, and I wondered what it would be like to be a part of a family. To have a mother and father, brothers and sisters.

Aunt Matilda's needles stopped, "What are you thinking of, my Lilly?"

She always knew when something was weighing on my mind, almost as if she could see my face.

"I was thinking about the village in the valley." I paused, "What do you know of it, Auntie?" I had asked the question a dozen times, and the same distant look came to her eyes each time.

"It is of little importance," she said quickly. "There are many people there. They are unkind, and only care about what they want. They judge and exclude anyone who wants something different from them."

The harsh, cold voice stopped. To any other question, she would respond slowly and with composure. What was it about the village that made her react the way she did?

Her voice broke through the evening silence, soft once again, "It is time we got to bed, little one." She often called me her 'little one' even though I was sixteen years old, and several inches taller than her own, stooped body.

I stood, "Yes, Auntie." I opened the splintered, wooden door. The air was musty, and the two foggy windows let in little light. On the far wall was a spacious fireplace with a cobblestone hearth where two wobbly rocking chairs sat. At one end of the room was the straw mattress that Aunt Matilda and I slept on, with a worn patchwork quilt spread across it. On the opposite wall were a few cupboards, and in the other corner lay a pile of wool, ready to be woven.

I walked into the little room. Aunt Matilda followed, placing her knitting on a small wooden table beside the door.

"Will you tell me a story, Auntie?" I asked after we had changed into our nightgowns and lay down on the thin mattress.

For as long as I could remember she had told me a story before going to sleep.

She smiled, and drew the quilt up to her chin, "Once upon a time . . ." Her old voice gently rasped, "there was a woman who loved books and learning and children. She was a teacher in a little school in a small settlement," Aunt Matilda paused, "A settlement that was beginning to grow. The teacher saw how things were changing. She saw the neighbors she had once known and loved, begin to change. They seemed to only want more; more business, more things, more wealth. The school teacher decided she would speak to each wife and mother in the settlement. She would help them see that the old ways were the best ways."

Aunt Matilda's favorite saying was, "The old ways are the best ways."

She continued with her story, "The next day, she went from house to house, explaining that money and riches, big houses, and new, fancy things were not as important as the peaceful, happy lives they were giving up."

Aunt Matilda's voice was weak with emotion. Why did this story mean so much to her?

I continued listening.

"The women refused to accept what the teacher said. She started keeping to herself and everything in her home stayed just like it had been before new inventions were brought to the settlement."

She spat out the word inventions like a mouthful of dirt.

"After that, the people of the town shunned the school teacher." Aunt Matilda's lips grew tight. "They would no longer nod when she passed them in the street. They would no longer invite her for dinner after church on Sundays. Eventually, they asked her to resign from teaching.

There was nothing left for her in that place. She could not stay there. She packed her meager belongings and left. She traveled up into the hills."

Her voice relaxed, "Up in the mountains, she heard a tiny baby crying." A half smile swept across her face, "She walked on through trees and bushes and came to a little cottage. Inside, she found an infant; pale and thin. She took the little one in her arms and cared for her from that day on."

June

I started from my sleep. I had dreamed of Jacob and the life we could have together, but then my parents' dominating presence had invaded that dream. If I married and left my home, I would be leaving Joshua.

I wiped the cold beads of perspiration from my forehead and moved the thin curtains back from the window above my bed. Stars still pierced the sky and the moon shone brightly. I would go to Jacob; I had to. He would understand that I couldn't leave my brother as a lone slave to my parents in order to be with him. I stood, careful not to wake Joshua sleeping on the mattress beside my own, but he was already awake.

He sat up quickly, "June? Are you going to see Jacob?" His wiry frame was a shadow in the darkness.

"Yes, Joshua," I answered. "But this is the last time."

I couldn't see my brother's face, but I knew he was frowning, "I thought you loved him! I thought you wanted to marry him."

I lowered myself to my own mattress so I could speak more softly, "I can't marry him, and leave you. I won't, and you know there's nothing you can do to change my mind."

"You wouldn't be leaving me," Joshua protested. "Jacob's the sheriff. Once you're married, he can get me out of here; and you can adopt me."

I paused for a moment. I hadn't considered that I could help Joshua by leaving more than I could by staying. He was right. Jacob would be happy to adopt my younger brother, and then we would both be rid of our parents' cruelty.

"I'll do it," I whispered then paused again. "It won't be long, Joshua. I promise I'll get you out of here as soon as I can."

"I know," he whispered. "I know."

I leaned closer to him, and we held each other for a moment. Then I left the bedroom, crept silently through the house, and stepped out into the night.

In half an hour, I stood in front of Jacob's door. That cabin had been my safe haven for seven months. I took a moment on the doorstep to let my pounding heart slow down.

I thought back to the day Jacob and I met.

I'd had an especially difficult week when we met. My father heard there was a man coming to the village who was offering a lot of money for any crop sold to him. It wasn't true, but my father thought it was; and he worked me and Jacob day and night. We barely slept or ate, and we worked for hours in thunderstorms, and burning heat.

The day Jacob and I met, I had gone into town upon my mother's request for sweet onions.

The afternoon was muggy and hot, and dirt

had turned into mud on my sunburnt face as sweat trickled down my nose and cheeks.

As I left the store with my bag of onions, I staggered beneath the heat on my way down the sidewalk. The lack of food, water, and sleep, along with the heat, had finally caught up with me. I collapsed. Everything went dark.

The next thing I knew, there was a gentle hand moving a cool damp cloth across my forehead and temples. At first, I was afraid I would open my eyes and find my mother there, but I knew she would never do such a thing.

My eyelids fluttered and finally opened. A young man looked down at me, startled when his gaze met my own. He pulled the cloth away from my head, and smiled shyly. "Hello," he said.

"Hello." My voice sounded weak.

"Father!" he called into the next room, "She's awake."

A tall, middle-aged man with dark hair and a scruffy jaw stepped quickly into the room. I sat up as he did, but the sudden movement forced my head back onto the couch as a wave of dizziness swept over me.

The young man sat down next to me, "Are you alright?" he asked.

"Yes," I answered, pulling slightly away from him. The older man took a seat nearby and reached to touch my forehead. I pressed my back against the couch. He looked confused, and lowered his hand to his lap.

He smiled after a moment, "I'm Carson

Plyer, and this is my son Jacob," he said. "He found you in the street and brought you here. We're both concerned for your health, Miss," he paused. "Can you tell us your name?"

I looked at Jacob's eyes. His face was honest and gentle. I didn't know why I liked his relaxed features, and open gaze, but I felt safe with him. Safer than I had ever felt before in my life. "I'm June Miller," I answered.

Suddenly, I noticed the slant of the light stretching across the rug on the cabin floor. "What time is it?" I asked quickly, dreading the answer.

Both men were startled by my abruptness. "Around supper time, I imagine," Carson answered.

"Oh, no," I stood quickly despite my throbbing head, "I have to go!" I looked around for my bag of onions.

"Your bag is in the kitchen, Miss Miller," Jacob said.

"Would you please get it for me?" I asked.

"Of course," Jacob hurried out of the room and brought the bag back in.

"Don't go yet," he said as he handed me the bag, "You need to rest. Just stay for supper, and then I'll take you home."

My eyes wouldn't move from his. I wanted to accept his offer. I didn't want to leave, but my parents . . .

"I can't. I'm already late with the onions."

Jacob frowned a little; his light blue eyes looked sad, "At least let me take you home. It's still hot and you don't want to faint again on your way."

    I bit my lower lip, "You can walk me half way."

Lilly

I woke up and stretched. Something was different. Aunt Matilda wasn't up. She lay beside me breathing shallowly. I touched her shoulder, "Auntie?" I whispered.

She stirred slightly, her eyelids fluttering.

"Don't you feel well?" I asked.

She turned her pale face to me, "No, dear. Prepare the medicines . . ." She coughed painfully, "I've taught you. Go quickly."

I got out of bed, slipped into my dress, found a sack for the plants I would gather, and saddled Shandra. That morning, the familiar trails held fear and uncertainty in the fog. Before long, I came to the Forest of Pines, as we called it, and jumped down to search the ground for herbs.

My hands trembled as I touched the plants, searching for the ones that would heal her. I had gotten sick several times, but I couldn't remember Aunt Matilda ever being sick.

I gathered every herb I needed, none of which I knew by name. Auntie had taught me to recognize them by sight. I ran back to where I'd left Shandra, remounted, and returned home.

I was soon boiling a soup of herbs and milk from the wild goat we had tamed. When it had cooled for several minutes I spooned out the leaves and poured the milk into a cup. I gave it to Aunt Matilda. She drank slowly and fell into a fitful sleep.

I repeated the steps, making more of the milky soup. I woke her up, and she drank it again. Over and over, I repeated the process, having to go out on Shandra to collect more herbs. This went on long into the night.

Sometime before dawn, she turned to me, "Rest now, my Lilly. I will be fine." She smiled feebly, "I will be better in the morning."

I agreed, lay my weary body down next to hers and went to sleep.

When morning came, Aunt Matilda wasn't better.

June

Silence enveloped Jacob's house. The door opened softly as soon as I reached to tap on its wooden planks. Jacob's smile sparkled in the filmy light of the moon. "What are you doing here, June? We hadn't planned to meet. Are you alright? Your parents didn't---"

"No. Jacob," I cut him off, and took a quick breath, "may I come in?"

Jacob moved his tall frame aside for me to enter and shut the door behind me. I spun around to him, "I have to ask you . . ." I stopped. Every feminine instinct told me not to say it, not to ask a man to marry me. It wasn't my place to ask; it was his. Yet, I knew he loved me. He'd said so dozens of times, and shown it even more, "Jacob, I know you love me, and I've told you how much I love you," I spoke quickly, "It's not the woman's place, I know, but---"

Suddenly, I was in Jacob's arms. I buried my face against his shoulder, but he pulled away and knelt on the ground. His smile was genuine, radiant, "June, I love you more than my own life. Will you marry me?"

Tears ran down my cheeks. I nodded, "Yes," I laughed, "Yes!"

I knelt down in front of him, and he took me in his arms again. He held me gently, and I knew he would never let me go.

Lilly

I got out of bed, careful not to disturb Aunt Matilda. I ate my breakfast quietly and prepared another mug of the milk. I touched her shoulder lightly. She tried to open her clouded eyes, "It's time for breakfast, Auntie. Can you sit up?"

She coughed then her voice rasped, "I can't." She paused, breathing heavily, "I will not be here for you anymore."

Tears flooded my vision, "You'll get better. You have to stay with me," I plead. "Try to drink it."

I moved the mug to her lips, but she only lifted a trembling hand to push it away, "No, my Lilly. Listen to me." She coughed, "Find a good home for yourself. Somewhere you can belong. It was . . ." Tears sprang to her eyes, "It was wrong of me to keep you here."

"What do you mean?" I asked, "Where would I be if not here? I don't understand---"

She tossed her head back and forth on the pillow, "I have kept you away from all else. The teacher in the story. Her name was Matilda, and the baby's name was Lilly."

The baby was me!

"I named you Lilly because you were just

like a beautiful flower, sent down from Heaven to cheer a lonely woman's life."

She stroked my cheek. "Go now. You'll find your way, my Lilly."

Those were her last words. I found myself standing in front of the house, gently stroking the rim of Aunt Matilda's spinning wheel. What was I going to do without her? I wondered how my heart could continue beating when hers didn't.

As a young girl, she taught me how to knit, how to grow a garden, and how to cook. I remembered the time I found a thick, red-covered book in her clothes chest. I asked her what it was. She'd explained what books were. And she told me about reading, and how people looked at the symbols on the page to learn new things. I had turned to her eagerly, "Auntie, will you teach me to read?" Her eyes glazed over for a moment before answering, "No, my Lilly." She smiled, "You have no need of people's foolish ideas."

My mind wandered to the story she had told me. How could that have been only two nights before? She'd been so happy, so able, so alive. What would I do now?

Aunt Matilda's words came to my mind, "Find a good home for yourself. Somewhere you can belong."

I knew what I had to do.

I found Shandra grazing, grasped her mane, and pulled myself onto her back. I didn't think of taking anything with me. I turned toward the narrow trail, lit only by the low, rising sun;

and set out to begin my new life. Shandra's steps felt heavy on the hard earth. I was leaving my home behind me forever.

June

Sunlight flowed through the white lace curtains on the kitchen window, our kitchen window. The smell of pancakes filled our home.

After marrying Jacob, he took me to a small home he had bought in the woods, not far from town. I loved the house from the moment I stepped through its sturdy wooden doorframe.

I heard the front door open and Jacob's heavy boots step across the living room floor. I turned to see him come into the kitchen. He smiled wearily. I dismissed the tiredness behind his blue eyes for a moment, as I skipped into his arms.

I smiled up at him, "Supper's ready."

His mouth curved slightly to smile back down at me, "Good. I started smelling it before even reaching the edge of town."

I laughed, "You did not."

"Yes, I did. Six people stopped me on my way to ask if I thought you made enough for guests."

I smiled again as I went to fix his plate.

After eating, Jacob pushed himself away from the table and sighed good-naturedly, "You did the cooking; I'll wash the dishes."

I placed my hand over his on the edge of the table, "Did you have a hard day?"

His tired eyes finally let down the mask of joviality they'd worked to hold during our meal, and he sighed. "Your parents came to see me."

I fought the urge to let out a sigh of my own. "They do that. Were they asking about Miriam again?"

"Yes," he answered heavily.

"Well, that's nothing to worry about, is it?"

"No," he hesitated, "but it reminds me of all we can't do for Joshua."

His words pricked at my heart, making it ache to comfort the brother I loved so dearly.

Would we ever be allowed to adopt him, to rescue him from my parents? My eyes went to Jacob, and my throat tensed as a familiar wave of fear ran through me.

I let out a long breath, "Joshua knows we try." Despair weighed heavily on my shoulders. "We try," I repeated quietly.

Lilly

When I got to the hilltop, I sat for a long time, looking down on the village. Where would I go? Where would I belong?

The early-morning wind blew my hair, and cooled my face. It continued down the slope of the mountain, into the valley. Distant trees moved and swayed against a faded blue sky.

"Go. Go now!" Aunt Matilda's voice seemed almost carried on the breeze, "Go now, my Lilly."

I urged Shandra forward, and we started down the mountain. When night came, I slept on the mossy ground and woke just as the sky was turning from black to a deep, velvety blue. The trail was barely visible when I started out again.

Nothing felt real to me. I didn't care about my stained and muddy dress, or that I didn't have any food.

After riding for several hours I noticed that the trees were thinning, the narrow trail broadened, and dirt showed through the worn grass.

Then, up ahead, I heard people talking. It made me nervous. I rounded a bend in the trail, and rode into the town.

June

Three years passed. My life with Jacob brought me more joy than I ever thought possible. They were beautiful years, yet not free of work, as well as worry over Joshua's plight. Thoughts of his escape from my mother and father's home plagued us day after day, year after year. Our joy never came from the absence of heartache, it was only deepened as we struggled through heartache together.

One sunny day, I ran into the jailhouse. Jacob had forgotten his lunch, and I hadn't realized it until two that afternoon. I smiled as he turned from the open filing cabinet. He laughed when I held up the basket. He ran over, wrapped his arms around me, and kissed me quickly. His eyes sparkled as he smiled down at me, "I believe I have the most extraordinary wife in the valley."

"Do you only think that because I bring your lunch, Sheriff Plyer?"

He pulled me closer to him again, "I believe I'd faint from exhaustion if I took the time to list every reason, Mrs. Plyer."

I smiled, and he snatched the basket from my hand.

I opened my mouth in mock frustration.

"Care to share my lunch, Mrs. Plyer?" He asked.

I raised my chin and turned my head, "If you insist, Mr. Plyer."

We both laughed.

After eating, he left to walk around town, and I stayed in the jailhouse to finish a blanket I was knitting for one of the cells.

Lilly

I was riding along the strange dirt trail under the sun in a state of delirium. I urged Shandra to the grassy edge, and she stopped. I slid down, afraid I might fall from her back.

From somewhere behind me came a low voice, "Miss? Miss?" The man ran up beside me, catching my arm just in time to save me from collapsing, "Are you alright, Miss?"

I grabbed his arm and leaned against him. He took me into a large brick structure and quickly put me into a chair.

I noticed another person in the room. They were talking to me; trying to keep me awake. I couldn't understand them. Then everything got quiet as the man knelt in front of me. Holding my head up in his hands, he leaned close to my face. He spoke in a clear, slow voice, "What is your name?"

"Lilly," I told him.

He sighed, "Okay, Lilly." He took a dark red berry from a plate that someone held out to him, "Eat this Lilly." He put the berry in my hand. I ate it obediently. He handed me several more, which I ate.

Relief flowed through me. I felt calm,

relaxed. I was so tired. I fell asleep sitting in the chair. This time, they let me.

June

The girl slept so soundly, so quickly. Jacob took her in his arms and carried her easily to a bunk in one of the cells. After noting the girl's bare feet and tangled curls, all I could see was her resemblance to myself. I took my work into the cell and sat in the rocking chair. I wanted someone to be there when she woke up.

Lilly

I awoke slowly, coming out of a deep sleep. I looked around the room. I was laying on a stiff bed. The walls, the floor, and the high ceiling were all made of dark, smooth stone. The bed was against the back wall; and at the front, was a long row of metal bars running from the floor to the ceiling.

Then I noticed a woman in the corner, sitting in a small rocking chair. She sat knitting, her needles clicking. She was young and wore a bright, flowered dress. She looked up as I studied her face.

She smiled pleasantly, "Well, look who's awake." She stopped her knitting. Her voice was soft and clear, "Are you feeling better now?"

I wasn't sure how to answer. I had never spoken to anyone except Aunt Matilda, but the woman was waiting for my reply.

"I feel a little better," I paused. "If you please, where am I?"

"This is the jail." The woman looked at me another moment, then stood abruptly, "I'll get Sherriff Plyer. He's the man who brought you here."

She went into the other room, and I heard

soft voices, then the man walked in, "Hello, Miss Lilly. I'm glad you're feeling better. We were worried. You nearly collapsed on the street last night. Would you like to try sitting up now?"

"I guess I would."

I leaned up slowly on one elbow. The man took my thin hand in his own and lifted me slowly. I swung my legs around and sat up on the edge of the bed.

"How does that feel?"

"It feels alright. I think I'll sit here for a minute."

"That's fine. Whatever you like." He brought the chair the woman had been sitting in over to the bedside, "Now, I'll introduce myself. I'm Jacob Plyer. I'm the Sheriff here. And you are Lilly . . ."

"Yes, I'm Lilly," I said.

"I know that, but what's your full name?" he asked.

"I . . . I don't know what you mean."

He looked shocked. His face relaxed before he spoke again, "What is it you don't understand?"

"I don't know what you mean. Lilly is my full name."

He seemed to be contemplating, "Never mind that," he finally said. "Where are you from?"

"I came from the hills."

"Did you not have food on your journey?"

"No, I haven't eaten for a few days."

"No wonder you nearly fainted. Is this your

destination then?"

"Yes, it is."

"Does your family live here?"

"No."

"Have you come to see someone?" he asked.

"No. I was only coming to the town, where I would be with people."

He thought for a moment, "Were you alone in the hills?"

My mind went instantly back. Back to the trees, the cottage, and Aunt Matilda, "No, I lived with my Aunt Matilda," I said, "She died the morning I left."

The man's face dropped, "I'm sorry," he said softly, "Wasn't anyone else there?"

"No," I answered flatly.

"I see," he sighed. "Well, why don't you rest a little longer, and then we'll find you a place to stay tonight."

The woman walked back into the room with a small platter that had different types of fruit on it. She smiled, "Here you go, Lilly. You can sleep more after you eat."

They both sat with me until I had eaten all I wanted.

Then they got up and left the room as I eased back onto the pillow. I heard muffled voices coming from the next room.

"Well, Jacob? Did she tell you anything about herself?"

"Not much. All I know is that she's from

the hills and she lived alone with her aunt who passed away a few days ago. She came here to be with people."

Everything would be okay. They were good people. I could rest.

It was morning when I woke up next. The sun was shining into a barred window high up on the wall. The woman from the night before walked in and smiled down at me, "Good morning, Lilly! You were sleeping so soundly last night we decided to let you stay here."

"Good morning," I said, sitting up slowly. "I'm sorry, but I don't remember your name."

"Oh, yes. That's because you never heard it. I'm June Plyer, the sheriff's wife. You can call me June."

"Thank you for helping me last night, June."

"It was no trouble, Lilly. Look what I brought you." She took something out of a big bag she had carried in. "A clean dress. I thought you might want to change before going out."

"Yes, I do. Thank you for bringing it to me."

She handed me the dress as I stood up. "After you change, we'll go to our house and have breakfast." She pointed toward a basin of water on a table in the corner of the room, "You can wash over there."

I put the dress on and went out into the room where June was waiting, "I'm ready to go," I smiled.

She smiled back at me, but then glanced

down at my feet.

"Where is it you said you were from?" She asked.

"The hills to the east."

"Oh," she said thoughtfully, then looked tenderly into my eyes, "Jacob told me about your aunt. I'm sorry."

"Thank you," I said, "and thank you for everything you've done for me."

She smiled. Her face was so kind. What was it about her that was so familiar.

We studied each other for a moment. She laughed, "We should get going. It's past breakfast time already."

We walked to the door and out into the street. The number of people passing by startled me. I stiffened and grabbed June's arm. She turned to me, "What's wrong, Lilly? Don't you feel well?"

"No . . . I just . . . There are so many people."

She looked at me worriedly, "They won't bother you."

I looked out at the sea of faces. How could she not feel the same? How could all of them not feel what I felt?

I couldn't say anything.

"We can talk about it later." I heard June say, amidst the bustle of the street, "Hold onto my arm. We'll go to the house where it's quiet."

We walked to Shandra. I had forgotten about her. Riding on her strong back made me feel more secure. She was all I had left of home.

Somehow, Shandra and I would make a home for ourselves, a place to belong, just Like Aunt Matilda had said.

A rope tied Shandra and June's dark brown horse together. I looked toward June's back. She was small and had long, curling brown hair, a quick step, and sparkling blue eyes. I realized that she looked very much like myself. Maybe that's why we looked familiar to each other. I guessed she was older than me, but not by so many years.

June

Lilly was different, not only in the way she seemed to be ignorant of many everyday conveniences; but her presence was different. She was afraid of people, but she seemed to trust Jacob and me.

I turned back for a moment to make sure the rope tying our two horses together was still secure. Lilly was looking lovingly down at her mare. She reached out to stroke its long white mane.

The resemblance between us was strong. It made me wonder . . . But how could it be? My baby sister had been left all alone. She was gone.

I dug my heel slightly harder into the horse's side. I wanted to get back home to Jacob.

Lilly

We had long since turned off the main road and headed out of town. We were on a long dusty road with fields and trees on either side. It felt more like home; I could breathe easier. The smell of morning dew rose into the air and birds sang in the trees.

We turned off the dirt road, onto the grass in front of a white house. Stepping inside, the smell of wood burning and food cooking made my already growling stomach feel even emptier.

"Jacob must have breakfast nearly ready," June said.

I followed her into the kitchen. It was spotlessly clean, and full of food.

Sherriff Plyer nodded when we came in, "Good morning, Miss Lilly."

"Good morning."

I sat in a chair next to June at the table. She spoke directly, "Lilly, I wanted to ask you what scared you so badly when we stepped out of the jail this morning. Can you tell me?

Her eyes were searching mine.

"I've never seen so many people before."

Jacob sat down, and put the pot of oatmeal on the table.

"What about your neighbors up in the mountains? Surely you visited sometimes."

"There were no neighbors."

June looked concerned, "You didn't live near anyone?"

"Before yesterday, Aunt Matilda was the only person I had ever seen." I paused. "You're the only other people I've ever spoken to," I said.

"We are?" June voice was strained.

"Didn't you have parents?" Jacob asked.

"No. It was just me and Aunt Matilda."

"What do you plan to do now?" Jacob asked.

"I suppose I'll find a cottage to live in."

He looked uncomfortable, and so did June.

"Is something wrong?" I asked.

"Well," June started, "It's just that, I don't think---"

"What June is trying to say is," Jacob's deep voice broke in, "you're not exactly allowed to do that."

"Not allowed? Why not?"

"The thing is . . . If you don't mind my asking; how old are you?"

"I'm sixteen."

Jacob's brow furrowed, "That's what I was afraid of. You see, children younger than eighteen must live with a legal guardian. What I'm trying to say is that you have to be adopted."

I looked back and forth between the two, searching for an explanation, "What does that mean?"

June looked pleadingly at Jacob, then turned to me, "Lilly, you're not eighteen yet. You need to be with someone who can take care of you."

"I can take care of myself. Aunt Matilda already taught me how."

June put her hand on my arm, "I'm sure she did, but . . ."

Jacob took over for her, "I'm sure you're very good at taking care of yourself, but there are laws. Do you know what laws are?"

"Oh, yes. Aunt Matilda explained to me about laws . . . how they work, I mean, but not what they were."

"Good!" Jacob smiled, "There's a law that says that anyone under eighteen years of age has to be adopted. That means you have to live with someone who has agreed to be just like your mother and father."

"You are saying that someone has to agree to let me live with them, just like I lived with Aunt Matilda."

"Yes," Jacob answered, "that's right."

I tried to smile back. But I couldn't imagine how anyone could take Aunt Matilda's place.

After breakfast, they took me back to the jail. Jacob sat at his desk with a small stack of papers and a quill. "You'll just need to answer a few questions." His eyes scanned the first page before looking up at me, "So, Lilly is your full name as far as you know?"

"Yes."

"Okay." He wrote something down on the paper, "You said you were sixteen; do you know what your birthdate is?"

"June twenty-third."

"Okay. Have you had all the childhood illnesses?"

I thought back, "Aunt Matilda said I was very sick once."

Jacob gave me an odd look, and wrote something else. "One more thing." He turned the paper around, pushed it toward me, and handed me the quill, "Just sign your name at the bottom, there." He pointed to a blank spot at the bottom of the page.

I looked from the paper to his face, "I don't know how."

"You don't know how to write?"

"No."

He took a long deep breath, "I'm sorry. I didn't know. Just put an "X" in the space."

"An 'X'?"

"Yes, it will work just as well."

"Can you show me how to write one?"

He nodded, "Here," he said, making two marks crossing over each other on the paper, "Just make one of these."

He handed the quill back to me. I dipped its tip into a small dish of ink, as I saw him do, and made the 'X', copying his exactly.

He took the paper and looked it over. Then he turned back to me, "I'm going to give this paper to the orphanage, and they'll arrange everything. You can stay here with June and me until the orphanage has a place for you. Would you like that?"

"Yes, thank you."

June and I spent the morning and afternoon cleaning the jail, and the evening waiting to hear from the orphanage.

The fire in the stove still burned dimly after we had eaten dinner. June was knitting absentmindedly; and Jacob sat at his desk, cleaning his gun, while I stared into the glow of the fire.

Jacob and June had explained that an orphanage was where young people lived while they waited for someone who wanted to take care of them. They said there's no reason to fear it, that a lot of children stayed there, but that's what worried me. I didn't want to be with a lot of children.

June looked up from her knitting at the clock on the wall, "Seven o'clock already."

Jacob looked at me, "Mrs. Bradly from the orphanage said she'd be coming by for you around this time."

My stomach tensed. I realized I was going to miss these two people who had been strangers just the day before. I turned to June, "Will I see you both again?"

"Oh, yes!" June sat on the edge of her seat. "Of course you will," she smiled.

"The orphanage is just down the road from here," Jacob added. "We'll see you all the time."

"Oh," I sighed.

They had both taken care of me. I wondered if others wouldn't be as kind, if they might be selfish or mean, like Aunt Matilda had always believed.

A knock sounded on the thick wood door. Jacob and June both stood to answer it. Not sure what to do, I stood and waited where I was. Jacob opened the door and greeted the woman, "Mrs. Bradly, thank you for working all this out so quickly. Please come in."

The woman was tall, and solidly built. Her large frame seemed to fill most of the little room. She wore a floral print dress, and her dark brown hair was loosely pulled back into a large, smooth bun. Her round face was full of determination, half hidden by some gentle quality.

"June!" The woman smiled, "It's been a while since we've seen each other. We've missed having you as a teacher. How have you been?"

"Just fine, and how are things at the orphanage?"

The dying firelight glowed against Mrs. Bradley's face as it softened in a wave of tenderness, "Oh, it's busy and chaotic. The children are happy and healthy for the most part. They spend every minute they can outdoors on these lovely autumn days." She paused to look at me then. Her dark brown eyes seemed to see straight through me.

I felt like dropping my own gaze to the wood floor, but didn't, "This must be Lilly." She came closer, looking down at me. "My name is Matty Bradly. I run the orphanage on the edge of town. Sheriff Plyer tells me you'll be staying with us for a time."

"Yes, Ma'am," I said, glancing down at the hem of my skirt.

There was a long pause, "Lilly?"

I looked back up into her large eyes. Her gaze encompassed me all at once, "Yes, Ma'am?"

"Are you ready to go?"

I didn't want to leave. I wanted to stay with June and Jacob. "Yes, Ma'am," I whispered.

She smiled, then turned to Jacob, "I'll be in touch. Come on Lilly, let's go see where you'll be staying."

She gave June a warm hug and Jacob a friendly smile, and then she went to the door. I didn't follow. How could I go with her, and leave Jacob and June? They were all looking at me.

June smiled and walked up to me, "You go with Mrs. Bradly. I'll come see you in the morning. Would you like that?" She wrapped her arms around me in a tight hug.

When she stepped back from me I tried to smile, "That would be nice."

Leaving Jacob and June, Mrs. Bradley and I stepped out into the dark, deserted night. The streets lay deep in shadow. Shandra was tied to a hitching post in front of the jail, along with a large bay colored horse. Mrs. Bradly swung herself onto the other horse, and I mounted Shandra. We started down the road without a word, and road until we came to the last building at the edge of town.

We dismounted, tied our horses, and stepped inside the heavy wooden door of the enormous red and brown brick building. The room was brightly lit with candles mounted on every wall. It had broad steps leading up to the second level and a large desk at the back of the room.

I stood there looking all around. My gaze finally fell to Mrs. Bradly standing beside me. She smiled, put a hand on my shoulder, and urged me further in. She marched up to the desk where a young woman was sitting. The girl smiled up at us. I stood slightly behind Mrs. Bradly, desperately wanting to hide from the eyes of yet another person. I had come to the town to be with people but still shrank from everyone I met.

"Hello, Margret. Thank you for keeping an eye on things while I was out." She turned to me, putting her thick arm around my shoulders, "This is Lilly. She's come to stay with us. Lilly, this is Margret. She'll show you around and get you settled in. I have some paperwork that needs my attention."

The girl bounced up from her seat, and floated over to me. She was short and slight. Darker curls than my own bounced with every step. She wore a light blue dress, a matching ribbon pulling her hair back. Her sparkling grey eyes were set in a fair face with blushing red cheeks.

She smiled, "The bedroom is up this way." She started for the wide steps leading up to the second floor.

I looked back at Mrs. Bradly. She was already deep in paperwork behind the desk. I wasn't sure I wanted to go with someone else I didn't know, but I turned to follow Margret. At the top of the stair case was a large, plain room with four doors along its walls.

Margret didn't stop walking until we reached the center of the room. Then she turned to me, "These doors lead to the bedrooms. That one's for the babies." She pointed to the door closest to the top of the stairs, then continued, "They sleep there until they are four, then they go to that one." She pointed to the next door. "They stay there until they turn nine, and children nine to sixteen sleep in there. And sixteen to eighteen is where we stay. This is the girls' building. The one next door is the boys'."

I looked at the door. So many people in so little space! I wondered what it would be like to live in there with all of them. I looked to Margret. She was studying my face.

"Lilly?"

I continued to look across at her. I saw she was concerned.

"Are you feeling well?" she asked.

"Yes, I feel fine."

"You haven't said anything."

"I'm a bit overwhelmed right now."

Her grey eyes glistened with sympathy, "I

understand. Most of us feel that way when we come here. I did, but I was only six at the time, so I got used to things pretty quickly." She smiled soothingly, "I made friends and felt right at home. You will too. It just takes time."

We stood quietly for a moment, then she said, "I don't remember ever seeing you. What part of town are you from?"

"I'm from the mountains to the east."

Her eyes lit up, "How nice!" She paused, her face softening, "Would you mind if I asked what brought you here?"

I thought she might understand about losing Aunt Matilda and leaving my home. She lived in the orphanage. She had also lost someone.

Before long, I had told her the entire story. Tears were coursing down both of our faces when I finished.

June

The ride back home that night was a quiet one. Jacob's shoulders heaved once again in a sigh. I could tell he felt as close to Lilly as I did. I was afraid to admit it to myself, but it was true. I wanted her to be with us.

Lilly

"Wake up, Lilly! It's time for breakfast!" Margret's voice broke into my dreams. A dream of being in the mountains, standing in front of the cottage. Inside, pots rattled. Aunt Matilda must be washing the dishes.

"Lilly, wake up!"

I opened my eyes to see Margret standing over me. I pushed the covers back and sat up on the edge of the bed. Then I remembered. The orphanage and . . . "Margret?"

"Yes, it's me," she laughed, "Get up, you sleepy-head, or they'll start without us!"

I stood up, and looked around the room. Each bed along the wall was empty and neatly made.

"Look at you!" Margret stood, looking me up and down. She was studying my slept in dress. "You can borrow one of my dresses after breakfast. For now, it will have to do. We've got to get downstairs."

We hurried out of the room and down the stairs. When we got to the bottom, we turned and went through a heavy, swinging door.

I didn't notice until the door had shut behind us, that the room was full of children.

There seemed to be hundreds of eyes, all resting on me.

Margret led me to a seat at one of the long tables and sat down beside me. On the other side, sat a young girl. She turned to me, and smiled, "Hello, my name is Meg. What's yours?"

"I'm Lilly."

Her young, expectant face lit up with an even bigger smile, "It's a pleasure to meet you Lilly. I'm ten years old today. How old are you?"

"I'm sixteen."

Her dark eyes widened, "You're six years older than I am. Did you come last night?"

"Yes."

"That's nice," she said, "You'll like it here. Mrs. Bradly takes good care of us. Margret and I are cousins." She and Margret exchanged glances.

I smiled at her, then turned my attention to Mrs. Bradly who had just stood from her seat at the head of the next table.

"Good morning, children." She swept the crowd with a gentle smile and continued, "After lessons today, we are going to visit the sewing factory down the road to learn about the different jobs there. I would also like to announce that last night we welcomed a new arrival." Mrs. Bradly pointed in my direction, and waited.

What was she waiting for? Then I felt Margret's hand pushing me up out of my seat. She leaned over and whispered in my ear, "Stand up, you silly!"

I rose to my feet. And once again, all eyes

turned to me.

Mrs. Bradly continued, "This is Lilly. She's sixteen, and has come from the mountains to the east. I hope you all welcome her and get to know her." She smiled at me and took her seat. I continued to stand. Margret and Meg both reached up at once and pulled me down.

Mrs. Bradly smiled at me again, then addressed the entire room, "Let's have breakfast, children."

Prayer was said, and Margret guided me to stand beside her in a long line of children. We each got a small bowl of oatmeal. Finally, something familiar! Oatmeal.

When breakfast was over, Margret grabbed my hand and dragged me back up the stairs and into the bedroom. We went to the foot of her bed where she opened a dark wooden chest and started rummaging through it.

"You're wearing one of my dresses today," she said, continuing her search. "Here it is!" She said triumphantly, pulling a light blue dress with a white collar and cuffs out of the trunk. She shook it out. "Not too wrinkled either." She held it up to my shoulders, smiled, and handed it to me. "The wash basins are in the corner, and here's my comb."

She smiled and left me alone, standing at the foot of the bed.

I took off June's wrinkled, slept in dress, folded it, and set it on my bed.

After getting the dress on and struggling

with the buttons, I went over to the wash basin on a small table at the end of the room. Margret walked in just as I finished combing my hair.

She smiled at me, "You look beautiful! Let's go down. We don't want to miss our lessons."

We left the room, and went quickly down the stairs.

This time, when we reached the bottom, we turned the opposite direction of the dining hall. There we entered another spacious room; though not as large. It was full of small desks with a chair at each one. Most of the children were already seated. It appeared that this room was for the older children.

Margret led me to two desks sitting beside each other. She told me to sit down in one, and she sat down in the other. "This is where grades six through twelve have their classes. The younger children are in the next room," she said.

"What's a grade?" I asked. She gazed back at me blankly. "Is something the matter?"

"No, no! It's just that . . . haven't you ever heard of grades before?"

"No."

"Oh! Well then, a grade is . . . It tells everyone how many years of school you've completed."

School was something I'd heard of. Aunt Matilda had told me many stories that involved children going to school.

"Oh," I said, "I understand."

Margret sighed in relief, "Good. Do you

know what grade you might be in then?"

"Well, I . . ."

At that moment, a woman with greying hair stepped up to the front of the room. All of the children stood at their desks. Margret motioned for me to stand too. The teacher looked the room over for a moment. Then we all sat back down.

The grey-haired woman continued to stand, "Good morning, children," she said in an authoritative voice. "Before we begin our lessons," I knew what was coming this time, "We have a new student in our class. Miss Lilly." She pointed toward me and waited for me to stand. I slowly brought myself to my feet, trying not to look at anyone in the room. "Welcome to our class, Miss Lilly. I am your teacher, Mrs. Pry. Before we get started, could you please tell me how old you are and what grade you are in?"

I looked up at her stern face, "I'm sixteen years old, Ma'am. I don't think I'm in a grade. I've never been to a school."

Everyone in the room seemed to hold their breath at once.

I looked up into Mrs. Pry's horrified face, "You haven't been to school? Ever?"

"No."

"Well . . . well, we'll just have to . . . We'll just have to . . . Can you at least read?" She finished loudly.

"No, Ma'am," I said quietly.

"Well! That is appalling!"

She leaned forward with her hands on her

desk. I continued standing, unsure what I was to do. Margret cleared her throat, bringing Mrs. Pry's blank stare to her, "Yes, Margret?"

Margret stood by her desk, "Perhaps, Mrs. Pry, Lilly should attend Miss. Cox's class until she catches up to the work we do here."

Oh wonderful, kind Margret! I wanted to hug her.

"Thank you, Margret," Mrs. Pry answered, "Yes, I think that would be best." She turned to me, "Lilly, you will have to go with the younger children until you catch up." Her shoulders were squared once again, and her face resolute, "Please follow me. I will show you to your classroom."

I left my desk with a look at Margret, and followed Mrs. Pry to a door on the side of the room. Through the door was another classroom, a mirror image of the first. Only the children seated at the desks were younger.

Mrs. Pry led me to a woman standing by the large desk at the front of the room. The woman was in her early twenties. She was tall and somewhat slim. She had straight, dark brown hair and green eyes.

"Mrs. Pry! How nice of you to drop in," the young woman smiled.

"This is not a social call, Miss Cox," she grumbled back.

"Oh? What can I help you with?"

"You may help me by taking this child off of my hands." She reached back, grabbed my arm, and pushed me almost nose-to-nose with Miss

Cox. "She's new to the orphanage and has never had any education at all."

"Oh!" Miss Cox took a step back, "Well, that's just fine. We're always happy to welcome new students to our class." She smiled at me.

Mrs. Pry let out a long sigh, "Good day to you, Miss Cox." She turned to go, but looked back at me as she left, "And good luck to you."

With that, she marched out of the room and closed the door behind her.

I turned to Miss Cox. She was smiling, "Well, Lilly, it's a pleasure to have you in our class. You can sit over there by Meg." She pointed to a desk next to the young girl I'd met at breakfast.

I went over and sat in the chair. Meg smiled at me, then turned her happy face to the front of the room. I did the same. Miss Cox began speaking to the class, "Alright, students. For those of you who know how to read, I want you to get out your arithmetic books, and give each other twenty problems. Everyone else, please get out your primers and trace the alphabet. If you need help, just raise your hand."

When everyone else had opened their books, Miss Cox knelt beside my chair, "Lilly, you and I can work together today."

"Alright," I agreed.

"Good," she smiled. "Do you know how to read?"

"No."

"You do know your letters though?'

She looked so expectant that I would know

my letters when, in truth, I had no idea what they could possibly be, "No, I don't."

"Oh, well we'll just have to learn them now, won't we?" she said with a smile.

"Excuse me, Miss. Cox, but what are letters?"

"Letters are what we write, and how we read books. Do you understand?"

"I think so. Are they the black marks on paper?"

"Yes, exactly! And you'll get to learn them now." She handed me a sheet of paper, "These are all of the letters. Once you learn their sounds, you'll be ready to learn how to read!"

She was very nearly beaming now. Ecstatic, it seemed, for me to learn the symbols. And suddenly, I felt like smiling too.

That morning I learned the first twelve letters of the alphabet. After lunch, I learned what numbers looked like, which was similar to the letters. Meg patiently taught me what each symbol meant and how to write it on paper.

Writing was like when I was little and would search for small dark rocks. They were soft and I used them to draw on larger rocks and boulders.

When mid-afternoon came, we were dismissed from classes. As promised, the older class assembled in the front room to go to the sewing factory. Miss Cox approached Mrs. Pry to ask if I shouldn't go along too, seeing as I was older, even though I lacked in academic subjects. I could see Mrs. Pry across the room as she was about to leave with the other children.

Mrs. Pry stiffened, "If she is so incompetent in academics, would you not suppose her to be equally behind in her sewing?"

Miss Cox's brow furrowed, "I know she hasn't learned to read yet, but---"

Mrs. Pry raised her eyebrows, and quickly cut in, "When she has shown herself to be proficient in the art of sewing, as you claim possible, only then will she have reason to see what one must do at the sewing factory. Don't you agree?"

"But I only thought---"

"Miss Cox?" Mrs. Pry cut in.

Miss Cox's shoulders drooped, "Yes, I suppose."

Mrs. Pry turned and led the group of children out the door.

Miss Cox looked defeated and tired. She must have been exasperated with Mrs. Pry, yet she never lost her temper. She came across the room and sat beside me on the bench where I'd been waiting, "I'm sorry you can't go on the field trip, but you can work on your sewing. Does that sound like fun?"

"That would be fine," I replied.

She smiled, "Have you sewn before?"

"Yes."

"Good! I'll get you a needle and thread, and some fabric." She smiled, "Wait here."

She went to a cupboard in a corner of the

large entry room, got the material, needle and thread, and came back to the bench, "This material is already cut into the pieces you'll need to make a dress. It should be about your size. You can wear it when you're finished." She handed me the bundle, "Do you need help getting started?"

"No, I know how to do it. Thank you," I said as she walked away.

Sewing was one of the first things I had learned to do as a young girl. The material Miss Cox had given me wasn't as smooth as Auntie's had been. Her thread had been finer than I could ever spin mine, even with her darkened eyesight.

After an hour, I had the bodice stitched together and had started work on the skirt. While I was concentrating, someone came and sat down beside me, "That's very even stitching, Lilly."

I looked up to see June's blue eyes sparkling over the dress coming together in my lap.

I smiled, "Thank you."

"We miss you at the house. How was your first day here?"

"It was fine."

"Good!" She said, "And how was school?"

"I'm not sure." I bent my head down a bit, feigning inspection of a row of stitches.

"That's alright Lilly. Things will get easier for you in school." She smiled hesitantly, "In the meantime, I've brought you a treat."

She set a small basket in my lap, lifting the cloth to show me what was inside. A warm, sweet smell drifted up to my nose. I reached down to touch one of the objects. They were about the size of my fist, with dark, sticky swirls throughout their golden surface. I had never smelled anything like it!

As I studied them, June leaned over, "Try one," she whispered.

I gently picked one up. It was soft, and dark syrup, that seemed to be made of some kind of sap, stuck to my fingers. I bit into it. The taste was gentle at first, but the sweetness increased as I chewed, and a sort of spicy flavor filled my mouth. It was delicious.

I looked up into June's smiling face, "What are these?" I asked.

"They're cinnamon rolls. Didn't your aunt ever make them?"

I shook my head, "I've never had anything like these. They're very good!"

"I'm glad you like them," she smiled. "I have to go now, Lilly. I promised to help a neighbor who just had a baby. I'll be back tomorrow," she said, standing to leave.

June

I had to pull myself away from Lilly's side. It was so hard to leave her, but I wasn't sure what to do yet. I gave her a hug, and left the basket of cinnamon rolls beside her.

I stopped on my way to the door to say goodbye to Lucy Cox. I had worked as an assistant teacher in the orphanage for several years, and we had grown close during that time.

She smiled as I gave her a hug, "How are things, Lucy?"

Her mouth turned up in a smile, but her brow furrowed.

"What's the matter, Lucy?"

"Her clear eyes moistened, and thin pink lips turned down, "Lilly isn't allowed to go to the sewing factory today because Mrs. Pry doesn't believe she can possibly be competent with a needle if she hasn't had proper schooling."

My heart dropped.

"I know she can sew, better than any girl I've seen," she continued, "Look at her."

I turned to peer over my shoulder at Lilly bent over her work.

I faced Lucy again, and placed a hand on her shoulder, "Don't worry. I'll see that things are *put right."*

I smiled one last time at Lucy and headed to the door.

As I reached for the knob, the door swung open, and Jacob stood in front of me.

Lilly

"Oh, Jacob! Not again?" June asked breathlessly.

He nodded, "I'm afraid so."

June sighed, shook her head, and walked past Jacob standing in the doorway. He took a long breath and went to the front desk where Mrs. Bradly was seated. He didn't notice me sitting on the bench near the stairs.

"How has your day been, Mrs. Bradly?"

She smiled, "Fine, Sheriff, and yours?"

"Just fine," he hesitated, "but I have a question I have to ask you."

"Ask away, Jacob," she answered happily. "I'll do what I can."

"The Millers came to my office this morning, asking about their girl again. I told them I would ask if you had any leads."

"Oh yes," she said slowly, "I remember the Millers. Who could forget them?" She laughed, "They ask about that girl every month or two."

Jacob shook his head, "They just won't give up."

"No, Jacob, I don't have anything for them this time, but I'll keep an eye out."

"Thank you, Mrs. Bradly." Jacob turned to

leave but noticed me sitting on the bench. He walked over smiling and tipped his hat, "Good afternoon, Miss Lilly."

I smiled, "Good afternoon, Jacob." It was good to see him again.

He sat down beside me and looked at the dress I was sewing, "Well, that's mighty fine needle work!" Then in a softer tone, he added, "Did your aunt teach you to sew?"

I looked down at my stitches. Aunt Matilda had taught me. She would have been proud to see the work I was doing on the dress, "Yes," I said. My voice sounded hollow. I didn't want to think of Aunt Matilda just then, "What were you discussing with Mrs. Bradly?"

"Oh, that." He grimaced, "It's June's parents. When June was eight, they had a little baby girl, but they lost her in the woods when she was two days old. They've always been rather vague about how that happened," Jacob paused, "Well, June and I know how, but we can't prove it," he said, "That was sixteen years ago. They come around every couple of months, hoping she's been found."

The story sounded intriguing. I'd always loved listening to stories, "But, how would you know if you found the girl?" I asked, "That was years ago."

"They say their baby had a birth mark of some sort."

"Is that unusual?"

He leaned back and smiled, "Well, a little.

They're all different."

"Oh. What did this mark look like?"

"It was a small one on the baby's wrist, slightly triangular and dark.

My eyes flew to the cuff on the sleeve of my dress, realizing that he was describing the mark hidden there.

I must be the Millers' lost baby! I looked just like June, her baby sister was lost in the woods, and Aunt Matilda found me in the woods. It was the only explanation.

My chest tightened as I realized that I had been uncared for and abandoned.

I looked into Jacob's bright blue eyes. I had to tell him. I didn't want to. My parents left me! Would I have to live with them? But if June was my sister, maybe I could be with her. I would have a family.

I looked back down at my wrist, slowly unbuttoned my sleeve, and started rolling it up. Jacob's forehead creased as he glanced down at the now exposed mark on my skin. It was a dark, triangular patch of skin. I looked from my wrist to Jacob's face.

All he could do was stare at the small mark. I was beginning to feel more frightened. I wanted to cover it up and pretend he never saw it, but I waited.

"That's the mark!"

We looked into each other's eyes, "I'm the baby," I whispered.

He studied my face, "You're June's sister."

I couldn't say anything.

He cleared his throat, "Lilly, we've got some things to straighten out. I'll let Mrs. Bradly know you'll be with me the rest of the day."

I put aside the dress I was working on and followed him over to Mrs. Bradly's desk.

She frowned when she saw Jacob's changed countenance, "Can I help you with something else, Jacob?"

"Lilly will be with me until further notice. She may not be back tonight."

With that, he took my arm and we ran outside.

Jacob's horse was tied next to Shandra. I patted her long, white snout before mounting.

We rode at a fast gallop down the road, toward Jacob and June's house. Once we got out of town, Jacob and I rode abreast of each other. The tension in the air settled on me, and my own thoughts suddenly turned to what had been revealed. I had a family, a sister. I stayed quiet for the rest of the ride.

We finally rode up and tied our horses to the hitching post in front of the house. We dismounted and Jacob took hold of my right hand, as if afraid to get near the small, black mark on the other side, and led me to the front door.

We went straight through the house into the kitchen. June was standing at the stove with a spoon in her hand and an apron tied around her waist. She turned, smiling as we came in. When she saw Jacob's face, her smile faded, "Jacob!

What is it? Is everything alright?"

"June," we had stopped just inside the doorway, "June, I'm not sure how to tell you this, but . . ."

"Go on, Jacob. What is it?"

"Sit down, June."

Jacob pulled out two chairs for June and myself, and threw himself into a third.

June looked from Jacob to me, her hands trembling.

Jacob took a breath, "I'm sorry to give you such a scare, June, but you won't believe what's happened." June's eyes searched Jacob's face before he continued. "I went to the orphanage for your parents this morning." He stopped, and June nodded, looking very perturbed. Anything having to do with the Millers was apparently disturbing, "Then I got to talking with Lilly." June's eyes darkened with every passing moment; her mouth flat, and tense. Once in a while she would look over at my face, but would quickly look back at Jacob.

When he had finished, she looked over and held my gaze for the first time since the story began. I looked into her earnest, blue eyes, the image of my own. My voice cracked, "I'm your sister."

Suddenly, we were standing, hugging across the table. We held onto each other's trembling hands. June's eyes were sparkling. Then, as we stood there, those eyes suddenly filled with fear. She looked down at Jacob whose face was already full of that same fear.

We slid back into our chairs.

"June?" I whispered. She and Jacob were silent, "June?" I tried again.

"Yes!" She started. "Oh, yes Lilly. There's something we need to tell you. It's hard for me to," she broke off.

Jacob took over, "June was born to the Millers, like I told you. They were not well loved in the community. People tolerated them, but it wasn't easy. They had been accused of robbery several times, and they were mean and deceptive people."

Jacob's eyes saddened, "When they had June, they didn't want her. They only wanted boys who could work for them. When June was three, Mrs. Miller had twins, a boy and a girl. They were frail, and both passed away within a few years."

June's face tightened and filled with unmistakable grief at the last sentence. Jacob put his hand over hers and continued, "One year after the twins' passing, when June was seven, they had a baby boy named Joshua. He was a strong, healthy baby. One year after his birth, they had a baby girl."

June glanced at me, and the corners of her mouth pulled up slightly.

"At the time of her birth, they were two days' journey into the mountains. Five days later, they returned claiming the baby was lost. Three years ago, they started coming to my office every couple of months asking if there was any information about their baby girl." He paused, "About you."

Jacob let out a breath, "The reason we're so concerned is because we don't want you with those people. We've been trying to get custody of Joshua since we were married five years ago, with no results. They'll put up a fight for you, Lilly."

"How did they say they lost me?" I asked.

"They won't say."

June

My eyes threatened to overflow again when Lilly turned to me. I let out a long breath before speaking, "I'll tell you what I can."

Lilly's light blue eyes watched me carefully. The tale of neglect and heartache would pain me to tell her. I knew she wouldn't miss a splinter of emotion or grief I felt in its telling.

"Father was gone for two hours. When he returned through the woods he was not even holding her little tattered basket." My voice seemed to be gone. I swallowed.

"I ran to him," I continued, "pulling at his hands, begging him to tell me where the baby was. It was no use, he shoved me away. We returned to our camp and stayed there three days before going home." I couldn't move my eyes from Lilly's, knowing they were the eyes of the helpless baby I'd spent two nights caring for, and then had ripped away from me. A tear rolled down my cheek, "I loved that baby more than I ever loved anything."

Lilly was looking steadily back into my eyes. Tears streamed down both our faces.

Lilly

I couldn't understand why I was crying. I felt something I'd never felt before.

"Do you want to know what you were named?" Jacob asked.

I looked at him. I didn't. I didn't want to know. I was afraid of the feeling that I had once been someone else, someone's daughter. A daughter they hadn't wanted.

But I did want to know, no matter how afraid I was. I looked back at Jacob's blue eyes, "Yes."

"Miriam." June whispered the name. The name of a baby from sixteen years before. The name I had been given by parents who hadn't loved me. The name of the sister June had thought was lost forever.

"We have to notify the Millers," Jacob said. "We won't let anything happen to you. We'll obtain your legal guardianship, if we can. June and I want you with us."

We were quiet during dinner. June kept looking at me as I spooned soup into my mouth. Was she thinking of my first nights as an infant, when she held me in her arms, and gave me water from her finger?

She loved me, but I had gone all of my life never knowing I had a sister who cared that deeply for me. Even if my parents hadn't wanted me, she had fought for my little life.

Thoughts tumbled through my mind as we washed the dishes and went into the front room to sit. The room was comfortable, with a sofa and two rocking chairs, all gathered around a stone fireplace and lit by several candles mounted to the creamy plaster walls.

Jacob lit the candles as June and I sat on the sofa. She turned to me, "You can stay here tonight, Lilly." She paused, her eyes softening further, and a smile spreading across her face, "We're sisters."

Something welled up inside of me. I squeezed her hand, "Sisters," I whispered.

I felt happy for the first time since Aunt Matilda had passed away. I felt like I was at home, where I belonged. I fell asleep easily that night.

June

The house was still quiet. Jacob was in the bedroom getting dressed, and I crept down the hall into the living room. It was filled with early morning sunlight.

Lilly was still asleep on the sofa, her eyes closed, her eyelashes softly brushing her lightly pink cheeks. She breathed deeply.

Lilly

I opened my eyes to sunlight pouring through the small curtained windows on either side of the oak, front door. Outside, dozens of birds sang in the tree tops, branches bobbing beneath their slight weight. Through the kitchen doorway, I heard sizzling in a frying pan; and the smell of pancakes wafted in.

The morning was lovely. The worries of the day before seemed to have melted away. The problem was almost forgotten, at least for a while.

After we'd eaten breakfast and seated ourselves around the table, Jacob spoke the inevitable, "I hate to bring it up, Lilly." He raised his hands in surrender, and June's eyes dropped to the worn table top.

I looked across at him, "Yes, I know."

He smiled weakly, "We'll have to call the Millers to come see you. They may not claim that you are their child, but we can't do anything until they say one way or the other."

I wasn't sure how to feel. The Millers were people June and Jacob obviously disliked. They hadn't seemed to care much for June or Joshua, and certainly not for the little baby they abandoned in the woods. They wouldn't care any more for me now than they had before.

June's touch brought me out of my thoughts. She looked into my eyes, "We'll be with you the entire time. You won't be alone with them."

I took a shaky breath. I wanted to be comforted, but I wasn't. I was afraid to meet them.

We took our horses and rode to the jailhouse again. When we arrived, Jacob called the Millers; and June sat down to wait with me.

Soon we heard the clattering of boots on the walk outside. We all stood, and Jacob crossed the room. He opened the old wooden door and a couple came in followed by a young man.

The husband appeared to be in his mid-forties. He was the height of the tallest horse's head, had a whiskery jaw, and seemed to fill the small room. His hair and eyes were light brown, and his nose seemed too small for his wide face.

The wife was round, much shorter than her husband, and had the same light blue eyes as June and me, along with curling, nut brown hair.

The boy, who stood meekly behind the two, was tall and wiry. His hands were large and the muscles on his arms were visible beneath his dirty, tanned skin. His hair and eyes were dark. I could see that he was overworked.

The man and woman looked over the room and their beady eyes came to rest on June's sturdy little frame. The woman spoke venomously, "June, do you not have a greeting for your mother?"

June's gaze never fell from the woman's. Both were equally firm, equally defiant, "Good morning, Mother."

The woman smiled a horrible, thin smile, "That's more like it." She turned to her husband, and he turned to Jacob, "What did you call us about, *Sheriff*?" He spat out the word, "We haven't done anything wrong, and that's a fact!"

Jacob answered with a coolness I couldn't have expected in response to such an angry tone, but I could see tension rising in his eyes "Mr. Miller, it has been brought to my attention," he took a moment before continuing, "It has been brought to my attention that your daughter, Miriam, may have been found."

The woman's hand flew to her mouth, "My baby!" She cried dramatically. "Where is she?"

June took my hand and everyone turned to me.

June

My family stared at Lilly. They stood still, their mouths hanging open in astonishment. There she stood beside me, nearly the exact duplicate of myself, obviously the daughter of my parents.

I watched my mother's beady eyes narrow. I couldn't guess what she was thinking. Here stood the daughter she had birthed, the daughter she refused to raise, and had abandoned. Now, she had to face what she had done, had to look into that baby's eyes.

She turned to our speechless father, "Karl!"

He continued to stare at Lilly, "Yes, I know," he said.

The family resemblance was plain; she was their daughter and my sister. Yet Jacob, not knowing what to do next besides display the mark, broke the silence, "We would like to show you the reason behind this assumption. Lilly, if you would come over here." He waited for her to walk over to him and our mother and father, but she stiffened, and I could see her throat tense.

My sister was horrified. And, why wouldn't she be? Our parents stood there, the parents she never knew she had. Yet, the day she learned of them, she also learned that they had left her to die.

Now they stood facing her.

I guided her over to Jacob, who smiled at me and took the other hand. That smile. He was protecting her, protecting me. He loved us, and would never let my parents hurt us again.

Then I looked across the room at Joshua. I knew he could see how my skin had healed from the cuts and bruises of overworking, and that I had the nutrition I needed. My skin had paled from the leathery tan it had carried from my childhood years of constant work in the sun.

Joshua held my gaze. There was no fear in his eyes, but all the love I had ever known from him. He knew I had been trying to save him. He gave me strength in that look; all the strength I could need that day, as I fought to save Lilly too.

Jacob cleared his throat, and gently pushed Lilly's sleeve up her arm, revealing her wrist and the mark. I looked at my father's dark eyes. They filled with satisfaction, still looking at Lilly's slight wrist.

Jacob's fingers were tense, his voice, deep and accusing, "Mr. Miller, is this your daughter?" he asked.

My heart leapt into my throat, looking away from my father to Lilly. Every emotion combined to form a tangible presence in the room: fear, agony, pain, anger, confusion."

Our father raised his eyes to Jacob, "Yes, Sheriff Plyer," he sneered, "this is my daughter."

Lilly

His eyes shifted to me. And there, the scene was suspended. Jacob's fingers were reassuring around my arm. June was tense beside me, and the man's angry stare bore down on my blazing cheeks.

Finally, the woman spoke, "Karl!" Her voice was shrill and irritated, "Karl!"

Mr. Miller turned to his wife, and she whispered something in his ear. Then his stony face turned to Jacob, "She'll be coming with us now." He reached and grabbed my wrist.

I looked at Jacob desperately. He wouldn't let me go with these people! Jacob answered my unspoken plea. His grip was firm around my arm. His other hand was pressed warningly against the man's billowing chest, "I'm afraid you won't be taking her today."

"She's my daughter. I have every right to take her whenever I please."

His nostrils flared wider with every word he spoke, and his grip pressed tighter around my wrist.

"I'm afraid the law can suspend that right," Jacob said.

Mr. Miller stepped closer to Jacob. I tried

to back away, but was firmly held between the two. They stood face-to-face above me.

"On what grounds?" He demanded.

Jacob jaw tensed, "On the grounds that you left your two-day old daughter alone in the woods to die, and that you neglected her during the two days you kept her. In addition, I intend to prove that you also mistreated your older daughter." At this Mr. Miller's eyes darted to June and back again. Jacob continued firmly, "And that you currently work your son too hard and feed him too little. We can't take him from you now, but we will."

The man glared down at Jacob, fierce and hateful, "You can't prove anything!"

Jacob was silent, staring back at the man with equal fierceness.

Suddenly, Mr. Miller ripped his hand away from my wrist and stormed out the door. I fell back a step and was against Jacob. He put an arm around me, and I steadied a little. The boy, Joshua, looked at Jacob with hope and fear before his mother grabbed his arm and they both followed Mr. Miller. A flicker of jealousy seemed to flash behind his dark eyes as his gaze passed over me.

I felt sorry for him. He was the one who had to spend every night and day with those two.

I looked back into his eyes, hoping with all my heart that he saw the anxiety I felt for him, my brother.

Jacob sent the judge a telegram, asking him if we could have the trial for the Millers as soon as possible. A reply came quickly. He would be there early the next morning. Then Jacob and June explained to me about judges and laws and courts and trials.

June and I spent hours knitting. She always kept a supply of yarn at the jail, and she taught me how to do it. She was a patient teacher. Each time I made a mistake, she would copy it in her own work, show me how to undo it, then show me how to do the stitch properly. It helped keep our minds off what the next morning could bring. Yet my mind seemed to wander between every stitch. I couldn't stop thinking of the trial, and every possible outcome.

Eventually, the day came to a close.

Lying on the couch that night, I thought about the look on Mr. Miller's face as he had glared at Jacob. I turned from side to side, each time seeing the image pass before my eyes. Fear didn't seem to be the right word for what I was feeling. I felt shocked, numb, as if I had stood for a long while in a snow drift, the lack of feeling nagging at me to go to the fireside, yet I couldn't.

There was something else in his face. Hatred, anger, vengefulness? Was Mr. Miller angry with Jacob for taking away his daughter? I couldn't imagine why he wanted me now when he hadn't wanted me before. Did he only want to have me in defiance of Jacob?

I was awakened early the next morning. June stood over me with the sunlight streaming through the windows in the front of the house,

"Good morning Lilly." She smiled, "I have breakfast ready. It's on the table."

I sat up in my borrowed nightgown, "I'll be right in."

She left the room and I put on the dress she had given me the night before. It was soft and white, and smelled like fresh air.

After washing my hands and face I went into the kitchen for breakfast. The hot cereal was delicious, but I didn't have time to savor it. Jacob sat studying several thick books all at once and June ate feverishly, lost in her own thoughts. All too soon, it was time to return to the jailhouse. The judge would arrive there to meet with us before continuing on to the court house.

I rode in a daze on the back of Shandra, through the early morning frost. The cold stung my cheeks, and I wished I was back at Jacob and June's home, sitting in front of the fireplace.

The key grated stiffly in the lock of the jail. The building was icy, and the coal was slow to start burning that morning.

Soon after we got there, a horse rode up with a black cloaked figure on its broad back. The judge walked in, as tall as the door frame, "Morning ladies." He tipped his hat to June and me before removing it. June hurried to take his hat, cloak, and gloves.

"Morning, Sheriff," he said to Jacob.

"Good morning, Judge. Can we get you some water?"

"Yes, thank you," he nodded to June, before

sitting down in the circle of chairs we had made.

For half an hour, he and Jacob talked of many things I couldn't hope to understand. The entire time, I watched the man's face. From what I understood, he would decide where I was to live.

Then he turned to me, his deep, attentive eyes searching mine, "And what do you think of all this, Lilly?"

"I want to be with Jacob and June."

He smiled sympathetically, "I thought you might." His eyes stayed fixed on mine a moment longer. Was that a look of recognition; something so familiar, yet distant. I wondered for an instant what it could be, and then the look was gone. He turned back to Jacob, "It's time we were going to the courthouse."

We went out and walked down the street. It had grown colder and overcast. The sky threatened snow, and wind whipped my skirt around my legs. I walked the short distance with my neck bent and my arms folded around me.

I would have to see the Millers again, have to face them, and watch June testify against them. I shivered and pressed my folded arms closer against my middle.

We turned into a tall red-brick building. Warm air hit me as soon we entered the double doors. We walked into a very large room with rows of benches, and thick white pillars supporting the high ceiling.

We went to the front and sat on the opposite side from the Millers. Judge Harris removed his black cloak and continued to the chair behind a desk at the front of the room. I sat between Jacob and June. Mr. and Mrs. Miller glared over at us. Joshua was hidden from view, sitting on the other side of his parents.

There was also a man seated beside Judge Harris's desk to write down everything that was said.

Judge Harris stood, "Let it be recorded that on the seventh day of November in the year of our Lord, eighteen hundred and forty-nine, we are gathered to settle the matter of guardianship of Miriam Miller as well as that of Joshua David Miller. Besides this, Mr. and Mrs. Miller are charged with neglect of their children."

He scrutinized the defendants in a glance, and took his seat, "Sheriff Plyer, you have the floor."

Jacob stood, "Thank you, Judge Harris. I would like to prove our accusations against the Millers by first asking June Plyer to tell her memories of Miriam's birth and subsequent loss." He turned to June and nodded, "Mrs. Plyer."

Jacob sat as June was sworn in. She recounted the story she had told me two days before. Judge Harris's expression was flat; but as June's story unfolded, anger flared behind his steady eyes and grew more intense as she told of the two long, sleepless nights she had spent with the baby. "Our father took the baby into the woods and came back without her. He wouldn't speak to me about the baby when returned. He acted like she had never existed."

June's voice stopped. I had been lost in the story. But then it was the Millers' turn to defend themselves. Mr. Miller stood and cleared his throat, "It is obvious that June's memory is severely distorted. But," he said in a lighter tone, "who can blame her? She was so young."

He laughed with some effort and began his version of the story, "In April of eighteen hundred and thirty-two, I took my wife and two children, Joshua and June, into the hills on a hunting trip. My wife was expecting, but a man has to provide food for his family. Doesn't he?" He feigned a silent plea for sympathy from the judge, but received a cold stare in return. The judge watched him from beneath thick, dark eyebrows.

Mr. Miller started again, a little less confidently, "And . . . after two days in the hills, my wife had a baby girl who we named Miriam. Giving birth was mighty trying for my Emmy, and I was exhausted from hunting. When night came, we gave Miriam to our little June to look over . . . in-between feedings. I told her to get us whenever the baby needed a feeding; but June, bless her heart, didn't want to disturb her poor Mother. Eventually she came to us, and we kept the baby in our tent the next night. In the morning, she was gone." He smiled shrewdly as he sat, appearing to be very satisfied with himself.

I glanced at June. Her hands were clenched into tight fists and her face had grown red. Judge Harris studied Mr. Miller's face for a moment,

"Thank you, Mr. Miller," he said shortly, then turned to me, "Will you please tell us about your time in the hills, and anything else you know about yourself?"

I looked at Jacob, sitting beside me, and tried to speak but couldn't. He smiled and urged me to stand. I stood there, looking nervously at the judge. He smiled kindly, "It's alright, Lilly. You have nothing to be afraid of here."

I nodded. I knew I had to speak, and that the judge, Jacob, and June would protect me if I needed it. "I lived up in the hills my entire life." My voice sounded thin and strange in the large empty room, "I lived with my Aunt Matilda. She was blind, but she could take care of us very well with my help. She got sick early last week. I did everything she'd taught me to do for illness, but she didn't get better." I stopped. It would be impossible for me to describe my thoughts or feelings about what had happened. I brushed a lone tear from my cheek and looked at the judge. His own eyes held tears in them. He waited for me to regain my composure.

"The night before she passed, she told about how she had found me. I didn't know before then. My Aunt Matilda went to the hills; that's when she heard me crying and found me in a cabin. The one I grew up in. She said I was thin and pale. She took care of me from then on. When she passed, I got on Shandra and rode to this place. June and Jacob Plyer saved me. I hadn't eaten for days and was fainting from hunger."

When I came to the end, the judge thought for a moment, then spoke, "The decision, in this case, is quite clear to me."

I had sat back down and could see Mr. Miller's chest bulging with pride.

"We had witnesses today, telling conflicting stories. These types of cases are commonly difficult to sort out, with many facts remaining unknown, in that each person's experience is only partially connected to the next."

He took a long breath.

"In this case, my reasoning is as follows. Miss Miriam Miller claims her aunt found her in a cottage, alone in the mountains. Mr. Miller claims the baby was lost in the mountains, but has not told us how this tragic loss came about. Mrs. June Plyer's testimony almost completely contradicts the story of Mr. Miller."

"I have come to three conclusions, if not questions." The judge looked to Mr. Miller, "How did the baby come to be lost? If indeed she was lost by some odd turn of events, why and how would she come to be in a cottage if not put there?"

Mr. Miller squirmed angrily under the frank gaze of Judge Harris. The judge continued, "And finally, what reason would Mrs. June Plyer have to deceive this court concerning the neglect of the child, and the mysterious loss of that same child, when all she has to gain from that lie is another mouth to feed?" He paused, "Therefore, I come to the conclusion that Jacob and June Plyer only have Miriam Miller's, or Lilly's, best interest at heart and would care for her very well. Taking all of the Miller's actions into account, Joshua Miller cannot stay in their custody. Therefore, I find Mr. and Mrs. Miller guilty of neglect and mistreatment of their infant, Miriam Miller, and their son, Joshua Miller. I hereby give full guardianship of both Joshua and Miriam Miller to Jacob and June Plyer."

June

A cool sensation washed over me. I couldn't believe my ears. Joshua and Lilly would be with me, with us, and never have to be the victims of our parents' insanity again! I wrapped my arm around Lilly, both of us smiling.

"As for you," the judge continued, speaking to our mother and father, "This crime was committed many years ago, and I can't arrest you for neglect." His voice was colder than the snow that had begun to fall, "I hereby order you to leave our town within the next thirty days. If you ever come back, I will see to it that you spend the rest of your lives in jail."

Mother gasped loudly, "Come, Karl! Let's get out of this place."

My father glared back at the judge's stony face before looking at Joshua one last time and standing. On his way past our seats he turned on us, "You haven't heard the last of me, Jacob Plyer," he growled. Then he looked at Lilly, "And neither have you, Miriam Miller!"

He turned away, without a glance at me; and then they were gone, with a gust of cold air flying into the room as the large doors shut behind them.

Jacob turned and put his arm around Lilly, "Don't worry," he smiled his ever-charming smile, "We won't be seeing him for a long time," he laughed, "You're going to be with us now." Lilly smiled, and turned to hug me. I smiled back, "My sister," she said softly.

I laughed, "Mine too!"

Lilly

While we were celebrating, Joshua had come up to Jacob. June and I turned to them. June smiled broadly and threw her arms around his neck, "Joshua!"

The boy smiled for the first time and turned to me. He put out a hand.

I took it, "Hello, Joshua."

"It's nice to meet you, Lilly." His brown eyes sparkled just as much as mine or June's.

A warm feeling rushed through me; it was safety and trust. I smiled back. I had a brother!

Over the next week, we all got to know each other as we arranged the few rooms of Jacob and June's home. Besides the kitchen and living room, there was a short hall with a door on one side and one at the end. The one to the left was Jacob and June's room, the one at the end was used to store food.

Jacob and June kept their room, but we had to move bags of grain, and baskets of dried fruit and vegetables out of the storage room and pile up quilts for me to sleep on. Joshua took my place on the couch in the front room.

Once my room was cleared of food and dust, had my makeshift bed in it, and curtains were hung over the window, it felt quite comfortable.

During those first few days we, spent a considerable amount of time sewing. Joshua only had the clothes on his back and I only had the dress June had given me.

Joshua would accompany Jacob every morning in his outdoor work while June and I worked in the house. When we finished the chores, and Jacob was home from town, we sat around the little table in the kitchen and ate and talked together.

I suddenly knew what a family felt like. There were moments I forgot we hadn't always been a family, moments I felt I knew the thoughts and feelings of the people around me.

Yet there were times when I would stand alone outside, on a starry evening and listen to the night animals stirring. The wind would blow the trees behind the house and on the mountain; and I was up in the hills again, standing in front of our little cottage, Aunt Matilda waiting for me inside, only the stars to keep us company.

It was pleasant remembering, and sad at the same time. The memory of nighttime in the mountains felt unreal at times, yet always like home.

One such night, while I was lost in my memories, Jacob came out of the house behind me. After a moment, he lightly touched my shoulder, "Lilly."

I turned to him, "Yes?"

He looked into my eyes for a moment, "Do you miss your home?"

I looked back into the eyes of someone I had so quickly grown to love. I took a breath and turned back to the stars, "Sometimes. On nights like this."

He stood beside me another moment, then asked, "What do you miss?"

"The air, the trees, and the night owl." I smiled slightly as tears blurred my vision.

He smiled and put his arm around my shoulders, "Let's get inside. It's cold out here."

We turned around, walked inside, and once again I was comforted by my new family.

Part Two
Family

Lilly

The first day of December rolled in with frosty splendor. The morning light sparkled and shone from every leaf and branch covered in thick hoar frost.

By noon the frost was gone, but the cold air would not go so easily. That didn't stop the boys from going out to the barn, or Mrs. Bradly from tripping up our walk to knock briskly on the front door.

June left me in the kitchen while she went to answer. I heard her energetic voice as I mixed the biscuit dough.

Then June walked in with a very excited Mrs. Bradly, "Lilly, it's so good to see you!" She said as she wrapped her arms around me in a smothering hug, "You and June are sisters!" She held me at arms' length and smiled, "I should have seen it all along. It shows all over you."

I smiled and joy seemed to grow behind her dark brown eyes, "You look wonderful. How are you settling into your new home?" she asked.

"Very well, thank you."

"That's wonderful!" She turned to June, "And I hear your brother is living here as well."

June's face lit, "Yes, he is. We're all settling

in wonderfully, and how is everything at the orphanage?"

The same tender look swept over her that I'd seen the day we met, "Oh, everyone is well and thriving."

"I'm glad," June smiled, "Why don't you stay for breakfast?"

"Well, I guess I can. That's all I'd be doing at the orphanage anyway."

Mrs. Bradly talked about what was happening at the orphanage throughout the entire meal. At one point, she turned to me, "You inspired something new at the orphanage, Lilly. We're going to look deeper into each child's family to be sure they don't have any relatives left."

"That would be good. Have you discovered any yet?" I asked.

"Yes, we have. We started with the older children. You remember Margret?"

I nodded, and smiled, remembering the bounce in Margret's step, and her lively, dark curls.

"So far, we've only found deceased relatives," Mrs. Bradley continued, "And only one that may lead somewhere. Margret and Meg had an aunt who lived here until sixteen years ago, and then she left and was never heard from again. Right now, we're trying to find out where she went."

Another story, one of family and mystery, "Why did she leave?" I asked.

Mrs. Bradley swallowed another bite of biscuit and drank from her water glass, "The woman was a teacher in the school for years. People say she went crazy. It started with a dislike of modern conveniences, but then it turned into rebellion against all new ideas. The parents didn't want her teaching their children any longer, so they dismissed her. One day, she just picked up and walked into the hills. No one here ever heard from her again."

Mrs. Bradly turned back to her plate to take another bite of gravy and biscuits, but my fork hung in the air. It was Aunt Matilda's story! The woman must have been her. Aunt Matilda was Margret and Meg's aunt! I had to say something. A month before that night, I wouldn't have had the courage to speak to Mrs. Bradley, but I had changed.

"Mrs. Bradly," I whispered.

She turned, a little surprised, "Yes, dear?"

I looked down at my plate and then back up, into her large eyes, "I know what happened to the woman that left."

Her eyes widened, "You do?"

"Yes," I breathed, "The night before Aunt Matilda got sick she told me how she had come to be in the mountains when she found me." I stopped.

"Yes?" Mrs. Bradly encouraged.

"It . . . It was the story you just told. Aunt Matilda was the school teacher."

I looked at June and back to Mrs. Bradly,

"Then your Aunt Matilda is actually Margret and Meg's aunt," she said. Then her eyes dropped, "She's gone too, their last living relative." She looked back up at me, the usual glow returning to her eyes, "But you're like a cousin to them. You must tell them about your aunt. They've been eager to find her."

"Why don't they come here for supper this evening?" June spoke up, "Lilly can tell them everything then."

Mrs. Bradly smiled, "Thank you. That would be wonderful!"

After we finished breakfast, Mrs. Bradly went back to the orphanage, and Jacob and Joshua went to the jail. Joshua had started going to patrol the town with Jacob each day. He seemed to enjoy helping him. June and I cleared up the breakfast dishes and cleaned the house.

We stayed busy the rest of the day. For supper, we cooked a roast with carrots, potatoes, and onions. I felt nervous to talk to Margret and Meg. They had never met Aunt Matilda, but it still might come as a shock to hear that their last living relative was gone.

I would soon find out. Jacob and Joshua had returned from town and the table was set with six places. Mrs. Bradly had only told them that we'd invited them to dinner; the rest was up to me.

They knocked on the door at five o'clock. I went to answer it, my heart pounding in anticipation of how the news would affect them.

I opened the door, and they both stood there in their long black coats and knitted mittens. Margret's grey eyes sparkled in the candlelight as they walked in. Meg took in everything with one gaze. Her face beamed, as it always did.

They both hugged me tightly.

Margret smiled, "We're so happy for you, Lilly!"

"Thank you," I smiled back, but I doubted I was beaming. Margret's expression shifted then. She saw my anxiety, and it looked like she would have asked about it if I hadn't stopped her by turning to hug Meg again, "It's so nice to see you!" I said to her, "Why don't you both come into the kitchen? Dinner is nearly on the table."

"It smells wonderful!" Meg said as she took my hand.

"It does," Margret agreed. She smiled at me over Meg's head. Her wonder at my anxiety was slightly hidden. I smiled reassuringly, and she seemed to relax a little.

June

Everyone talked and laughed. It felt as if Margret and Meg were part of the family. After we finished eating, I knew it was time for Lilly to tell them why they had come.

Her eyes swept around the table. I smiled, Jacob caught her gaze, and Joshua nodded, all encouraging her in some small way. I knew it would be hard for her to tell them that the woman was gone, that she had passed before they even had the chance to meet her; but most of all, it would hurt Lilly to recount the loss of the only person she'd ever known as a child, the woman who had raised her.

She turned to Margret and Meg, "We invited you here because I have something to tell you."

Margret looked as though she had been expecting something already, and Meg was subdued for a moment. We could all see the tension on Lilly's forehead and hear the strain in her voice.

"I know what happened to your aunt. The one Mrs. Bradly has been looking for."

Both girls' eyes widened as she continued with the story. Lilly explained to them more about her life up in the hills, and what their aunt had been like. "She loved me, but never showed it much.

I knew that deep down her feelings toward me were most tender, even if her manners weren't."

I finally grasped more of what Lilly's existence must have been like. I could see her with her aunt, sitting on the porch of a small, dilapidated cabin high up on the mountain top, never knowing what happened in the world that lay below her. Even if the town and its people had been visible to Lilly, she wouldn't have had any idea what they were like, or how people behaved or got along or existed together.

I looked at her thin cheek bones, at her jawline and arched eyebrows; then I looked into her blue eyes, moist with grief.

Lilly

I stopped and looked into the faces of the people I loved, and that loved me. Their eyes were all wet with tears, sparkling in the candlelight.

I looked into Margret's eyes. They glistened with something more than tears. She knew. She had lost her parents. Her understanding told me that what I was feeling was alright. I had struggled with so many emotions in the past weeks that I didn't know what to do with. But there, sitting across from me, was someone who understood.

Meg smiled, "I'm glad you knew our aunt, Lilly."

I sighed. Everyone smiled, and the mood lifted as we talked about other things.

I hugged Margret and Meg when I walked them out. Margret's eyes and mine were filled with tears. She blinked them away, "I can only imagine what that must have been like for you. Losing her, and then coming here all by yourself."

But she was the only one who didn't need to imagine how I felt. She had gone to the orphanage when she was six.

I hugged her again, very hard, "Thank you, Margret. I needed you here tonight."

"I needed you too," I heard her say over my shoulder.

We held each other at arm's length, "I'll come visit you," I said.

"That would be wonderful, wouldn't it?" she said, turning to Meg.

Meg beamed, "Oh, yes! Absolutely come see us!"

We hugged again, and they turned to walk away. We waved for as long as we could see each other.

When I stepped back inside, everything else was just the same as it had been the past four weeks, but I wasn't.

Aunt Matilda had taught me how mean and unfeeling people were. She had never told me what it was like to connect with another human being, to be hugged by a sister, to take the strong hand of a brother.

Why hadn't she told me those things? If she had ever been close to anyone, how could she have left the town? Is that why we never hugged, never laughed, why she had never taken my hand in her own?

Joshua sat down quietly beside me on the couch, "What are you thinking about?" he asked.

I shrugged, coming out of my thoughts, "Different things."

"Oh." He took a moment to look into the fire burning in front of us, "I'm sorry for everything you've been through."

I looked at him, "Thank you, Joshua. You

know, it's been easier to get through things with a big brother here."

"Thanks," he smiled. "I like having a little sister too."

I smiled back. We sat quietly, gazing into the flames. "Joshua?" I said.

He looked at me, "Yes?"

I pondered for a moment, "My aunt . . . She always told me how mean people were."

I paused, thinking, "That can't be true. I know there are people who are unkind, like the Millers, but what about you and Jacob and June, Margret, and Meg?" Tears rolled down my cheeks, "Why did she tell me those things if they weren't true? Was it all a lie?"

"No, no." He slid closer, and put his arm around me. "She wouldn't want to lie to you."

I looked up into his face, "Why do you think she told me those things, and never taught me how to read, or brought me to visit the town?"

He looked back into my eyes, and waited for several seconds before answering, "Some people," he started slowly, "some people have different ideas from everyone around them. I think your aunt misunderstood her friends. She thought they were rejecting her when it was really just her ideas about change."

I took a breath, "I wish she hadn't been afraid of new ideas. I wish our lives could have been different. It was a good life, but something was always missing."

"Have you found what was missing?"

"I think I have."

He smiled. I rested my head on his shoulder and closed my eyes. He understood me; my entire family did. My family!

December rushed on, and with its close, came Christmas.

"You're going to love it!" June beamed across the table where we were peeling potatoes, "There are lights in every window, people baking cookies, and the Christmas tree!" She clasped her hands close to her heart, and threw her head back in rapture, "Oh, the Christmas tree!"

I laughed at her theatrics, "What's a Christmas tree?"

"It's a pine tree you bring into your home. You place candles on the branches and string popcorn all around it, and the smell of pine fills the house. You'll love it!"

The next morning Jacob and Joshua brought a freshly cut pine tree into the house, and set it in the corner of the living room. That night we made popcorn and threaded the pieces on a long string. Then we draped it around the tree. June brought out a box of candles in small silver candle holders.

We fixed them on branches all around, and lit them. When Jacob blew out the other candles in the room the tree glowed as if dozens of stars had been caught in its branches. The house was peaceful that night; the night they called Christmas Eve.

After breakfast the next morning, we sat

around the tree as Jacob brought out several packages wrapped in cloth. He handed one to June, one to Joshua, and one to me.

I looked at it, "What's this?" I asked.

All three of them looked at each other in surprise.

"We forgot to tell her why we celebrate Christmas!" June laughed.

Jacob and Joshua laughed with her.

"What is it?" I asked, "What's so funny?"

They only laughed more. Finally, June caught her breath, "I'm sorry, Lilly. We told you we put up a tree and light it on a day we call Christmas, but we didn't tell you why we celebrate it, or about the gifts people exchange."

Jacob took over, "At Christmas we celebrate the birth of Jesus Christ."

I looked confusedly at him. I didn't understand. Why would we celebrate the birth of someone we didn't know? Who was this man whose birth the whole town celebrated?

I asked, "Do you know this man?"

"You haven't heard the story?" Joshua asked.

"No. I . . ." I started to reply, then remembered something. A story Aunt Matilda told me a long time ago, about a man who was born in a barn, a man who healed and served everyone around him.

"I remember a story," I said slowly, "My aunt told it to me when I was little. Over the years she told that story less and less, and eventually stopped. One time, I asked her to tell me again, but she never did, and I forgot about it."

"Each year, we give gifts to the people we love, just as men who loved Jesus Christ gave gifts to Him when He was born," June explained.

Jacob got a book and read the story I'd heard so long ago, about a baby who was rejected at the inn before His birth, and rejected many times after; a baby whose birth we still celebrate.

When he finished the story, I listened as they sang a song about the night of His birth. Then it was time to open the packages we'd been given. June opened hers first. It was two new knitting needles, and a bundle of yarn. She gave Jacob a new hat, and Joshua a thick, bound book.

Once again, the desire to be able to learn from the pages of a book swelled inside me.

June turned to me, "Open yours, Lilly. I think you'll like it."

I looked down at the bundle in my lap, and unfolded the cloth around it. Inside was a book! I looked up at June's face. Didn't she know I couldn't read?

She knew my thoughts right away, "Oh! Don't worry, Lilly. You don't have to know how to read already. This book will help me teach you!"

I smiled, "You're going to teach me to read?"

She nodded enthusiastically, "Yes!"

I couldn't wait to get started.

Jacob and June had another surprise for Joshua and me that night. They told us while we were sitting in the front room after supper. June had been beaming all day, and Jacob had a bounce in his step as he went about his daily chores.

"We have something we want to tell the two of you," June said.

"What is it?" Joshua asked. He must have noticed the change in them as well.

"We've given it a lot of thought, and we want to know what the two of you think of our adopting Margret and Meg," Jacob said.

I looked at Joshua, his expression reflected my own look of surprise. Then we smiled. We each knew what the other thought of that. We knew how it felt to need a loving home. There was a bond between us. We'd felt that same bond with Margret and Meg the night they were here. They had become a part of our family in the short time we had spent together.

June

It was all settled. We would go to the orphanage the next morning, and return with our entire family.

I noticed Lilly as we rode into town; she didn't shy away from the people on the street. She seemed more at ease. She had changed; this was her home.

We tied our horses in front of the orphanage and walked inside. Mrs. Bradly jumped up as soon as she saw our little group walk in.

"Sheriff! June! It's so wonderful to see you all!" She hugged me tightly, "What are you doing here?"

My smile felt impossibly wide, "We're here to adopt Margret and Meg," I said.

Mrs. Bradly's eyes widened, "That's wonderful, June! It's so perfect, so natural! I couldn't have planned it better myself." She ran over to the desk and got some papers out of a drawer, "Come here. All you have to do is sign these papers, and you can take them home."

Jacob and I followed her and signed the papers on her desk. "It's all just so perfect!" she said again.

I smiled at Jacob. We had a family, one we

hadn't imagined having just weeks before! How had we been so lucky, so blessed, to have so many to love and care for come into our home?

Mrs. Bradly filed the papers and told us to follow her to get Margret and Meg. We went to the door of the first classroom. Mrs. Bradly opened the door and we all walked in.

Mrs. Pry stood at the front of the class. She had been saying something about the importance of silence during class time when the door opened and she stopped, mid-sentence.

"Good-morning Mrs. Pry," Mrs. Bradly smiled, "I'm so sorry to interrupt, but I need Margret." Margret stood quickly, pushed her chair in, and bounced over to us. She hugged Lilly, then smiled widely at me. I couldn't wait to tell her!

Mrs. Bradly smiled again, "Thank you, Mrs. Pry."

We followed Mrs. Bradly across the room, through the next door.

The atmosphere in the next classroom was noticeably lighter. As soon as Miss Cox laid her brown eyes on Lilly, she stopped what she was saying, ran over, and hugged her tightly, "Lilly! I've missed you!"

Lilly's acceptance of affection would have surprised me from anyone but Miss Cox. I had known her since Jacob and I had married. She had gotten me out of my hard shell against people, now she had done the same with Lilly.

Lilly hugged her back. She looked happy to see her again. "It's good to see you too!"

They smiled at each other for another moment before Miss Cox turned to Mrs. Bradly, "What can I do for you, Mrs. Bradly?"

"Sorry for the interruption, Miss Cox," Mrs. Bradly gave her a friendly hug, "I'm here to get Meg." She winked and Miss Cox understood right away and turned to Meg, "You're excused to go with Mrs. Bradly, Meg."

Meg hopped out of her chair and ran over to us. Miss Cox gave her a hug before we left the room.

We passed back through Mrs. Pry's classroom, with her scowling at us all the time, and out to the front desk. When we got there, Mrs. Bradly turned to Margret and Meg, "I have wonderful news! The Sheriff and Mrs. Plyer want to adopt you!"

They quickly turned to me and Jacob, their eyes brimming. I smiled, "Will you come with us?"

Margret didn't answer. She just stepped up to me, and threw her arms around my neck. Meg ran to join us. When we stepped back from each other, Margret turned to Lilly. She reached out and hugged her tightly.

Lilly didn't say anything; she just smiled in that way of hers.

Lilly

It only took a couple of minutes for Margret and Meg to pack their few belongings. They didn't have their own horses, so Meg rode on the back of June's horse and Margret and I rode on Shandra's back.

The morning had come alive in the time we'd spent in town, and the snow in the air didn't sparkle quite so much with the sun shining from straight above. My voice broke through the stillness, "I'm glad we're going to be family now."

Margret giggled softly, "I know you are." Then she sighed, "It will be wonderful to live out of town. I've always lived in town, even before I went to the orphanage."

I grimaced, "I don't think I would like that, so many people and houses all around."

"I can tell," she said, "I can also see how much better off you are since living here," she added.

"You can?" I asked.

"You didn't used to want to talk."

I smiled. It felt good for someone to notice an improvement. I did feel different. I felt like it was fine to be myself, and to let others see it, at least at home. It was a good feeling.

June

That night we added more quilts to the pile on the floor of the bedroom Margret, Meg and Lilly would share. The next morning, when Jacob and Joshua went to town, there were four of us left to do the cooking and cleaning.

Margret knew how to do everything, and she did it all very well. She cooked biscuits, ground wheat, mended socks, brought water from the well, and dusted the living room. She enjoyed every minute of it.

When the work was finished for the day Margret came up to me, her dark curls bouncing on her shoulders, "How about we go sledding? There's plenty of daylight left, and the snow is perfect!"

I smiled, "I think we could do that."

"Oh really!" Meg cried, running into the room, "Can we go right now?"

I shrugged, laughing, "I don't see why not," I looked to Lilly, "How does that sound?"

She looked confused, "I don't know what you're talking about."

Margret and Meg and I all looked at each other. A wide grin started across Margret's face, and spread to Meg. We had some fun ahead of us. I smiled too, "What do you say, girls? Do you think we ought to show her?"

Meg nodded, "Let's go!"

We hurried Lilly to the front door where we put on our coats and mittens. We didn't tell Lilly anything about what we were doing or where we were going. I grabbed the sled from the barn before we ran into the woods behind the house.

Lilly

We walked for several minutes, the three of them whispering and giggling all the way. We came out of the trees at the crest of a hill and stopped.

"What are you waiting for?" I asked.

"Nothing," June said, "This is it."

"What is it?"

June dropped the large wooden thing she'd been carrying in the snow, seated herself on it, and pushed the ground with her feet. She suddenly slipped down the hill. She went faster and faster.

I turned to Margret and Meg, "Sledding! It's sliding."

June had reached the bottom and was walking the sled back up the hill. Meg called down to her, "She figured it out!"

June doubled over, and we all laughed.

When she got to the top of the hill, she placed the sled on the ground in front of me, "Your turn!" Her eyes twinkled above her red nose and cheeks.

"Okay," I sat and gathered my skirt beneath me.

I looked down the hill and felt a flutter in

my stomach. Before I could protest, Margret gave the sled a push. My heart raced as the wind bit at my chapped cheeks. The sled stopped as the ground leveled at the base of the hill.

I stood at the bottom and looked up to see three figures waving at me. I grabbed the sled and ran up the hill. I was out of breath when I got back to them. After Margret and Meg went down, we walked back through the trees. By the time we got home, the sun was low in the sky.

June turned to me as we walked in the door, "Lilly, can you go to the well and get the water for supper tonight? Jacob and Joshua will be home soon. And this evening, you and I can have a reading lesson," she smiled, "So hurry back!"

"Oh, and Lilly," Margret turned to me, "I was thinking I could show you how to make sweet rolls after your reading lesson tonight."

I smiled, "That would be wonderful! I'd love to make sweet rolls."

"Good!" Margret smiled, removing her cloak.

I started on the half mile walk to the well, the crusted snow crunching beneath my feet. The afternoon sky was a clear faded blue with wisps of clouds here and there. I would learn to read! And I would make sweet rolls! I had a family. I had a good life, and nothing was missing.

Visions of sweet rolls formed by my own hands, passed before my eyes; Jacob and Joshua coming in the door, their mouths watering from the smell drifting out of the kitchen, June's eyes dancing with praise.

Suddenly, someone grabbed me and tied a cloth over my mouth! I tried to scream, but I fell to the ground, and hit my head on a large rock jutting out of the snow.

June

I stood in the twilight on the front porch, looking across the yard and into the surrounding woods. Jacob and Joshua had gotten home half an hour before. The day had been so wonderful! Life was good. Jacob and I were beginning to build a family; first with Lilly and Joshua, then Margret and Meg, and now . . .

"What are you thinking about?" Jacob gently placed a hand on my shoulder.

I lay my hand on top of his, "Our family," I answered.

He smiled, "It's really grown these past couple of months."

"Yes," I smiled.

I felt the cold breeze through my coat and wrapped it more closely around me, folding my arms against my ribs, "Don't you think Lilly should be back by now? It'll be dark soon."

"Did she go to the well?"

"Yes, but she's been gone for so long." I turned to him, "I hope she's alright."

He smiled, "I'm sure she is. It takes a long time to get to the well and back, longer in the snow."

I frowned, "I guess so."

Jacob's eyebrows tensed. He looked in the direction of the well, "I'll go meet her on the path," he said and started away, "We'll be back soon. Keep dinner hot. We'll be cold." He smiled again and disappeared among the trees.

I turned and went inside. They'd be back soon. I'd finish dinner with Margret. She was quite a help in the kitchen and wanted to cook dinner herself that night, but I needed something to occupy my mind. I felt uneasy.

Lilly

Everything was dark around me. I was surrounded in some kind of cloth, bumping around, like I was in the back of a wagon; but how could that be? I was in the woods headed toward the well, but now . . . I didn't know where I was.

The wagon came to a stop, and I heard a muffled, angry voice and footsteps in the snow. Someone opened the sack and pulled it down from my head, and there were the dark eyes of Mr. Miller!

I blinked several times and tried to speak, but a cloth was tied tightly over my mouth. "Is she alive?" Mrs. Miller called from the front.

"Of course she is, Emmy!" he hollered. "I knew she would be," he mumbled and quickly retied the sack and got the wagon moving again.

In the dark sack, I was finally regaining my senses. My head ached from where it had hit the rock. It took some effort, but I was able to get my hand up to my forehead. I could feel half-dried blood around a deep cut. My fingers were wet and sticky when I pulled them away.

Then I remembered Mr. Miller telling Jacob that he hadn't heard the last of him.

My head hurt more with each jolt of the

wagon, and the darkness around me grew deeper. My hope was in the fact that they would have to stop for the night. We couldn't keep going in the dark.

When the wagon did stop, I waited for someone to let me out; but neither one of them ever did. I don't know where they slept that night, or if they even built a fire. If they did have a fire, none of its light or warmth penetrated to where I was. My legs wanted to curl up even further than they already were, but my knees were already tight against my chest.

The soreness from my cramped position soon faded as my limbs numbed in the cold January air, and I finally fell asleep.

Bump. Bump. Bump. I woke up being tossed from one side of the wagon floor to the other. I could tell it was daylight but had no idea how far we had gone. I tried to keep from rocking too much. My legs were still stiff and numb. I wondered if they'd ever regain feeling.

Hot tears ran down my frozen cheeks. What would happen to me?

June

"Lilly!" My voice rang through the black forest, mingling with the voices of others searching in the night. I ran, calling again and again. I wanted to cry, but there was no time. I blamed myself. I should have gone with her. I shouldn't have sent her out there alone.

We had searched for hours.

When Jacob had gone for Lilly, he discovered that she had never made it to the well. He had found the water bucket in the middle of the path, empty and dry. He ran back, frantic with worry, and Joshua suggested we follow her tracks in the snow.

The tracks ended abruptly about halfway to the well. At that point, the snow was all turned up. There had been a struggle. I nearly fainted when I turned around and saw a blood-stained rock sticking up out of the snow.

Jacob caught hold of my arm, and pointed off into the woods. There were more tracks, larger ones. We followed them and they led us to where a wagon had been stopped in the snow.

Even with dark closing in around us, we could see the wheel ruts heading into the hills.

Lilly had been kidnapped! I felt like my

heart had dropped, and become as still as the untouched snow on either side of the wheel ruts. My hands trembled. I didn't have to wonder who had done this terrible thing. My father's threat to Jacob had not been an empty one.

Jacob ran home and rode to my parents' house, just outside of town. They were gone, along with their covered wagon and many of their belongings. We had been searching for nearly eight hours. The sun would be up soon. My feet and hands had been numb for hours, but I didn't care. Getting Lilly back was the only thing that mattered.

The search party met back at our house just as the sun came up. Joshua, Margret, Meg, Mrs. Bradly, and Judge Harris were there, all wet and freezing from the long, aweful night in the woods.

"Thank you for coming, Mrs. Bradly, Judge Harris, we've done all we can here today." Jacob spoke dejectedly. "The fresh snow that fell during the night covered their tracks. I'm going to get word to every town within a hundred miles. They'll be caught soon enough. We all better get some sleep now."

Judge Harris told Jacob he would send word out for him, and that Jacob could stay home for the day; he would take care of things in town.

We thanked him before going inside and dropping into bed.

Lilly

It must have been supper time when they finally stopped, and I heard snow crunching as someone came around to the back of the wagon. I wanted to call out but felt it wouldn't matter if I ever spoke again.

Mr. Miller jumped up into the wagon. He opened the sack, pulled me to my feet, and untied the cloth over my mouth.

My legs burned. I was afraid they were broken! But it wasn't only my legs. My arms, back, and head, every part of me, felt as if it was shattering.

I couldn't keep myself up and fell onto Mr. Miller. "Stand up girl!" he flared, "You're as stupid as your half-witted brother and sister."

I stood as well as I could, not daring to fall again. Mrs. Miller came around the wagon to look in, "Hurry up, Karl. We're about to meet the wagon train."

"I'm tryin', Emmy. The girl can barely stand on her own two feet!"

"Well, make her. She's got to be walking when we meet up with the others," she hollered back.

The others?

Mr. Miller grabbed my arm and dragged me out of the wagon. We jumped down and landed in the snow in front of Mrs. Miller.

She put her fat hands on her hips, "Well, you better not be any trouble," she huffed, "You hardly look worth the trouble we've spent on you already." She turned to her husband, "Let's get going Karl, or they'll leave us behind."

They both went back to the front of the wagon. No one was watching me, and I wasn't tied up. Suddenly, I realized I was free! I could turn and run and never see my two captors again.

I looked back up the trail we had just come down. We were one day's wagon ride from home; but I hadn't eaten since the day before, and that was a long way back without any food. I remembered all too vividly my days without food when I left the mountains. Wouldn't being hungry for a few days be better than going with the Millers? But my mind found another obstacle. Besides the lack of food, I didn't know the way back.

I turned and followed their wagon fearing they would do even worse things to me and my family if I did get away. I would go with them and protect my family, but I would escape and make it back to the ones I loved. Someday.

We were at the base of the mountains. The trails in the foothills were wider with occasional breaks in the trees where we could look off to either side of the trail. Soon after starting to walk, I heard the sound of another wagon approaching, and we stopped.

Mr. Miller looked around the wagon at me. I had been behind them, and was just coming to a stop near the back.

He grimaced, "Clean your face off with some snow. There's blood all over it."

The wagon started forward as his face disappeared again. I bent down and scooped up some snow in my already frozen fingers and scrubbed it into my forehead. The rubbing brought the cut back to my attention. My pulse pounded behind it, and the snow falling to the ground was stained with blood. I rubbed it with fresh snow two more times, and then I couldn't take anymore.

Mr. Miller turned to me one last time just as a wagon rolled onto the path in front of us. The people in the wagon, a large young man with his mother and father, looked back at us as we followed them.

As we drove, another two wagons joined us on the path. Soon after, we came to a wide snow-covered meadow. There was one more wagon waiting there. All the others stopped in a semicircle surrounding that one.

The man in the center wagon stood on his seat, "Ladies and gentlemen, we are about to embark on a great journey to Gold Country." He spoke loudly, "The sooner we get started, the sooner we find our fortune. We'll have plenty of time for introductions later. So, let's get underway."

The little man sat down and pulled his wagon in front of the rest. The one behind his was a couple and their young son. They nodded to me as they passed us to get in line on the trail. Next, came the older couple and their son. We were behind them and last was a young couple. They didn't even acknowledge our presence as they took their place in the back.

Snow started to fall as we got started. A great journey? Where was Gold Country? I looked ahead of us. How far would we go? I felt cold and alone. The wagon wheels and horse's hooves crunched in the snow. Everything else was silent.

We went on until the sun sank below the trees ahead of us.

The group formed a circle with their wagons, and started their cooking fires. I stood in the shadows by the wagon while Mr. and Mrs. Miller sat near the fire. Mrs. Miller had cooked some sort of runny soup for dinner. It smelled rancid. I couldn't have eaten even if they had offered it to me. I wondered if they ever would ever offer me any, but I was too tired to worry about it then.

Every muscle in my body ached, and my numb feet would barely hold me up.

When the Millers were finished with their supper, they came around the back of the wagon. Mr. Miller stopped before climbing in after his wife, "You can sleep in the front, under the seat." He reached inside and pulled out a grey wool blanket, "Here."

I thought for one moment how much I wanted to be on a soft, comfortable mattress, but I was so exhausted that I knew I could fall asleep anywhere. Mr. Miller started to climb into the wagon and I turned to leave.

"And one more thing," he said. I turned back to him, "Call us Mom and Dad."

I couldn't imagine ever calling them anything, but I nodded in agreement and turned to the front of the wagon. I climbed in and curled up under the seat. The wood was hard, and the old blanket he'd given me smelled as rotten as their soup had. I wished I was home. I could imagine what we would have been doing that night; Margret would be smiling at me across the fire-lit living room while June taught me letters from the alphabet. We would be together and happy and warm. I sighed, desperate to be with them.

I fell asleep quickly despite the blanket, the hard wood, the bitterness of the cold air, and my own thoughts.

Morning came quickly. I woke up in the dark to Mrs. Miller dragging me from beneath the wagon seat. She spoke angrily, "Come on, girl. We've got to get going!" She pulled and prodded me until I stood unsteadily on the ground.

The snow had deepened overnight and came nearly up to my knees.

The wagons were already lined up as they had been the day before, with the couple and their son ahead of us and the young couple behind. We started to move ahead in the snow and woods. I had no choice but to lift my feet high, and keep up the best I could.

The walking was hard that morning. Half melted snow clung to my feet, legs, and skirt. Numbness climbed higher with every mile.

The sky hid behind grey clouds throughout the morning, but I knew it must have been noon when a stale piece of bread flew around the wagon and into the snow in front of me. I stopped and looked to the front. Mr. Miller's head popped around, "Well pick it up and keep moving!"

His red face disappeared again. After the first two slow bites, feeling started to return to my stomach. By the end of it I felt hungry all over. The bread had only served to awaken the want of food. I almost wished I hadn't eaten it at all.

The cold worsened as the sun sank that evening. My legs had long since gone numb under my frozen skirt and leggings. The melted snow in my shoes made my feet feel even colder. I considered taking my boots off and going barefoot; at least then my feet would be free of the heavy snow that clung to them.

Just before dark, they stopped the wagon train again. Everyone joined the tight circle, one family's camp meeting the next.

I stood beside the wagon again, looking on as Mrs. Miller prepared supper. Mr. Miller came back from gathering firewood and dropped the brush beside the flame his wife had just lit. Then he looked at me, "What are you doing, girl? You're a part of this family. Help your mother with supper. Get a scoop of barley for the soup."

They both watched as I rounded the side of the wagon and opened the barrel secured to it. I brought a scoop to the pot over the fire and dumped it in. Mrs. Miller resumed stirring, and Mr. Miller climbed into the back of the wagon.

I backed away again, trying to get as far from Mrs. Miller as I could. I couldn't stop my hands from trembling. Partly because of the cold, but largely from my dread of being spoken to by that man. Fear and despair wrestled in my heart.

I looked away from the fire and across the snow covering the trees and hills around us. My shoulders slumped as I thought of my home becoming further and further out of reach.

From the next camp over I heard a voice, and my eyes traveled from the snow-covered landscape to the family with the young son. The mother came out of the wagon and walked to where her husband stood over a large, steaming pot. She smiled as she slid an arm around her husband, "Thank you for making dinner. That nap did me a lot of good."

"I'm glad," he smiled and returned the embrace, "Cody and I had fun doing it." He nodded to the young boy sitting on a log, whittling by the fire.

The mother smiled at the boy, "Are you ready for supper, Cody?"

He looked up, "Yes, Ma! I could eat the whole pot!"

They all laughed as the boy ran to get the dishes and came back to his parents. While he filled his bowl, the man and his wife looked up. They caught my gaze and smiled.

My heart slowed its rapid pounding and my hands were still for a moment. Then I thought to smile back. It seemed so long since I had smiled! It felt good. Peace seemed to reach out from their camp and wrap itself around me. I felt safe.

"What are you doing, girl?" Mrs. Miller's voice was loud in my ear, "Don't just stand in the snow! There are other things to get done."

I stepped forward to get the wooden spoon from Mrs. Miller and stir the soup. I could still feel the couple's eyes on me. When I looked up again, I saw their anxious faces.

June

"Three days! How could no one have seen them in three days?"

Tears filled my eyes. I paced back and forth in the front room, and Jacob sat in an armchair by the fire. Joshua, Margret, and Meg had gone to town to do the shopping.

Jacob looked tired. "I don't know what to do next," he sighed. "Every town for over a hundred miles has been alerted. We've tried following their tracks, but the snow just keeps falling." He sighed again and lowered his eyes.

I sat down gloomily in the chair beside his, "You're doing all you can."

Three whole weeks passed without any word.

I pulled my heavy coat closer around my shoulders as I pushed against the wind whistling along Main street. I soon came to the jailhouse door. I went in quickly and pushed it closed behind me.

Jacob came across the room and put his arms around me, "You must be freezing."

I buried my face in his chest, "I am."

He took my coat and led me to the stove.

We sat in two wooden chairs, and I started

to unwrap the bundle I'd carried with me, "I brought lunch."

"Good! I'm ready for it," he smiled, "Where are the kids?"

"They decided to stay home instead of braving the cold."

He smiled and nodded. Most people in town were staying indoors. The winter had become exceptionally cold, much more than any I remembered.

Judge Harris walked in just as we were finishing our lunch, letting a cold gust of air blow through the little room. I hadn't seen much of him since the night of Lilly's kidnapping.

"Good afternoon, Judge," Jacob greeted him.

Judge Harris smiled and took Jacob's hand, "Afternoon, Jacob."

He shook my hand, then addressed Jacob again, "Have you heard anything?"

Jacob shook his head. I looked at the judge. His sadness suddenly struck me. I watched his face as he continued to speak. "I'll be leaving for the west in the morning. A lot of the wagon trains heading out to Gold Country have been plagued with Rocky Mountain fever. I'm going to help the trains that don't have their own doctor."

Jacob smiled and nodded, "They'll be lucky to have you. Safe travels."

They shook hands again, and Judge Harris went back out into the cold. Jacob and I stood there, watching him go. I had to know what he was thinking. He seemed to care so much about what happened to Lilly.

"I'll be back in a minute," I called back to Jacob as I ran out the door and into the cold.

The doctor was walking quickly down the road. I rushed after him, "Doctor! Judge Harris!"

He turned, and waited for me to catch up, "What are you doing? You shouldn't be without a coat in this weather."

I hugged my trembling arms to my ribs as I tried to catch my breath in the frosty air, "Judge, you seem deeply concerned about Lilly?"

His eyebrows raised, "She's very young. I'm concerned for anyone who can't fend for themselves."

I studied his face; his eyes, his furrowed brow where snowflakes landed and melted, "Nothing more?" I asked.

His eyes rested on my face before answering, "You're very perceptive, Mrs. Plyer." He stared at the ground for a moment before going on, "We all have experiences that influence what we do in the future." He paused and his large brown eyes looked into my own, "Something in my past leads me to try to help your sister."

He held my gaze. Tears ran down my cheeks, "Thank you . . . whatever it is."

He nodded, and turned away.

I turned quickly back to the jailhouse. Jacob was waiting for me at the door. The cold had already stiffened my muscles and cooled the tear on my cheek. I wiped it away and walked into Jacob's arms and back inside, thankful for the good *people around me.*

I wondered if there was anyone Lilly could turn to; wherever she was.

Lilly

"Can I help you with that?" A small, clear voice spoke from behind me.

I had staggered, once again, under the heavy weight of the iron kettle I'd carried the last two days of our journey. I turned to see who had spoken. The young boy from the family I had noticed early in our trip was waiting for my reply. The top of his blonde head just reached the level of my chin.

As I looked at him, he asked again, "Could I carry that for you, Miss?"

I didn't want to make him feel bad, but I didn't want to let a little boy carry my load, "Are you sure you could manage?" I asked.

He smiled, marched up to me, and swung the handle of the kettle onto his little shoulder, then he started forward to catch up with the wagon. His step was light and his back barely bent under the heavy load. I started forward to keep up with him. He looked over at me and smiled.

How could he be so much stronger than I was? I looked down at myself. The coat I had on, from nearly a month before when I'd been sledding, was poor protection for walking all day in the cold. It was dirty too. And I was quite a bit thinner after so little food and miles of walking each day. I wondered how I looked to the boy.

"How old do you think I am?" His clear voice cut into my thoughts.

I looked over at him, "Ten years old?"

His eyes lit up, "Yes! You're very good at that!"

I couldn't help smiling, he was so impressed with me.

"What's your name?" he asked.

"Lilly," I paused. "I've heard your parents call you Cody."

"Yes, that's my name."

After several more minutes he spoke again, "Why do your parents let you carry this pot when it's too heavy for you?"

I didn't quite know what to tell him. He'd asked a straight forward question and deserved a straight-forward answer. It was a good question too, one I could have asked myself.

"They . . . wanted more room for my mother to rest in the wagon."

I watched the ground and pretended not to notice the look of astonishment on Cody's young face. We walked on in silence for several more hours. As the wagons circled for the night, Cody handed the heavy kettle back to me, "I'll see you," he said, skipping off to rejoin his parents.

I let the pot rest on the snow as I watched him run into his parents' arms. As they let him go and started to set up camp for the night, they nodded at me. I almost smiled. Maybe there was hope for me. At least there were people I might be able turn to.

Over the next two weeks there were many times Cody carried my load. Cody was Mr. and Mrs. Duckson's only child. Mr. Duckson was a blacksmith; but business had been bad in the east, so he decided to join his brother in California. Even if he didn't strike gold, there would always be work for a blacksmith in a place like that.

Seeing Cody's family reminded me every day of my determination to get back home. But for now, I accepted that my life was with Mr. and Mrs. Miller. I didn't resent them for what they had done. They were evil people; nothing I could do or say would change them. I stayed out of their way as much as possible and rarely thought of them during the long, cold days walking beside the wagon. And they only spoke to me when they wanted something done.

I was never as warm as they were. I never had as much food as they did. No breakfast, a piece of bread at noon, and a bowl of watery soup for supper. I walked while they rode. The only thing that didn't weaken from the harsh conditions were my legs. The miles I walked each day wouldn't let them.

One day, around noon, Cody turned to me, the heavy pot on his shoulder, "Lilly, I'll keep going while you go get some food from my parents. You could use it."

My mouth quickly began to water. I was

convinced that Mrs. Duckson's cooking was the finest in the entire train. The smells coming from their wagon were sweet, warm, savory, or spicy, but always comforting, "I suppose I could," I said slowly.

He smiled, "Just climb into the back of the wagon. My mother is expecting you."

I smiled and turned to go. Suddenly an angry voice bellowed from behind me, "Miriam!"

I stopped and swung around. The wagon stopped. I waited, and Cody waited, still holding the iron kettle. Mr. Miller jumped down and crunched through the snow to where I stood.

He towered above me in silence for several seconds before speaking, "Where are you going, Miriam?"

My tongue felt stiff, but I managed a few words, "I wouldn't have stayed away long."

"You're not allowed to go," he answered then looked at Cody, "And you're not allowed to speak to this boy, or anyone else. Do you understand?"

My throat was tight, and I needed to cry; but I only nodded.

He continued to look down at me, "Tell me you understand."

I swallowed, "I understand," I whispered. Tears finally overflowed, burned my cheeks, then cooled in the freezing wind.

Mr. Miller took the iron kettle from Cody and placed it in my hands. I let it rest on the ground and stared into it in silence.

He turned back to Cody, "Get out of here, boy. Go back to your own wagon."

Cody glanced at me before running back to his parents. Mr. Miller got back in the wagon and it started moving again. Cody had carried the kettle nearly every step of the way, but now I was left with no relief.

I let the kettle's bottom drag in the snow behind me as I continued forward.

My arms ached that night, as I curled up beneath the buggy seat. The cold, relentless wind blew through my blanket and I brought my knees closer to my chest. Just before my eyes closed in sleep, I heard a painful fit of coughing somewhere in the camp.

I hoped it wasn't Cody or his parents getting sick, but I couldn't ask Cody in the morning. I could never speak to any of them again. I tear rolled down my cheek once again for the loss of the only friends I would have on the journey.

In the morning, I learned that the young man and his mother were ill as well as the young couple that had been traveling behind us.

For four days, the sick lingered in a state of unconsciousness. It had circulated throughout the camp that the young man and his mother would soon die.

The morning was one of freezing sunshine and sparkling snow. While getting the breakfast fire started, Mr. Miller stormed toward the wagon, "Miriam! Emmy! Come with me."

Mrs. Miller came around the back of the wagon, "What is it, Karl?" Her voice was harsh.

Mr. Miller answered flatly, "Mrs. Willis is dead. We're going to her burial."

Mrs. Willis? I had never heard the woman's name before. I wasn't grieved by her passing, only troubled that someone could be living one day and gone the next. Tears coursed down my cheeks and my legs refused to move to follow the Millers. I was grieving for Aunt Matilda. It had been so long since I'd been with her, so long since I'd thought of her. Could I have forgotten her?

Mr. Miller turned to me, "Come on, girl. We haven't got all day."

My hands flew to cover my face, and I ran to the back of the wagon. I couldn't go with them! I couldn't watch them bury a woman I had seen living only the week before.

They must not have thought it was important for me to attend, because they left me. A half hour later Mrs. Miller climbed into the back of the wagon and chased me out. As I jumped down, the wagon lurched forward and I landed on my knees in the snow. I stood quickly and started walking.

As we pulled away from camp, we passed a low mound of upturned dirt and snow. A rock lay at the head with letters engraved on it. I couldn't read them, and I didn't want to. I wanted to pretend it had never happened, pretend I wasn't here, traveling away from my home and family with these people.

I turned my head until the lonely grave was far behind.

June

Firelight filled the living room. The end of March, and still no relief from the cold. Earlier that week, we had finally accepted that we wouldn't find Lilly. No one from the surrounding towns had seen her, and it had been so long.

We were forced to decide that accepting her loss was the only hope for our family to move on. Lilly wouldn't have wanted our hopes shattering with every sunset.

Sitting in front of the fire, I was starting on a blanket for the baby that would be coming in five short months. My mind had not been able to rest for so long but finally seemed to quiet itself that night.

Margret walked in just then. She'd been out getting wood from around the side of the house. She smiled gently as she set the wood down on the hearth, hung her coat, and curled up in the chair beside mine.

Her grey eyes rested on the work in my lap, "What are you working on? I love the color."

I looked up and smiled at Jacob. We hadn't told anyone yet. There had been so much going on.

Margret looked back and forth between us, "What is it, you two?"

I turned back to her, "I'm going to have a baby!"

Margret's eyes lit up, "You're going to have a baby? June!"

I laughed, "Yes!"

I held up the blueish-grey strip of blanket, "It is a lovely thread."

She nodded approvingly. She was silent for a moment before going on, "Do you think . . . I mean, would it be alright with you if . . ."

"What is it, Margret?"

Her eyes were grave and intensely grey, the same color as the blanket in my lap. Her eyes always darkened when she was troubled, "Would it be alright if I used Lilly's books to help Meg with her reading?"

My hands continued working as my eyes went to the primer and several beginner books stacked on the mantle. I blinked a tear away and cleared my throat, "That would be fine."

I looked back at her. She got up and walked over to where the little stack of books lay above the fireplace.

She picked up the book on top and opened the cover. It was the most advanced reader we'd gotten for Lilly. I wanted them to be used and loved, but would it make my heart ache as much every time I saw Meg using them as it did that very minute?

Margret seemed to feel my gaze and turned around. I looked away quickly, but not fast enough to hide my pain. She set the book down, "These are *a little simple for Meg. I'll have to find something more advanced for her to read."*

After one last smile, she went into the kitchen. Margret always knew just what to say, and she knew when a book that was gathering dust needed to be placed back on the shelf. Maybe someday the pain would go away; but for today, I had my family to comfort me.

Lilly

The entire camp was affected by the Rocky Mountain fever. Those who didn't have it were either getting over it, caring for someone who had it, or trying to avoid catching it.

The man in the lead wagon had contracted the fever, and the train was laid up for three days. It had been two weeks since the first case. This morning, nearly everyone was gathered around the lead wagon, waiting to hear whether he had pulled through.

Finally, the canvas flap was slowly pulled back. The man dragged himself to sit on the buggy seat, his voice barely audible in the morning stillness, "Life has triumphed!" The crowd kept silent, but a feeling of relief was almost tangible. The man spoke again, "Who lives or dies on this trip is not up to us, but to the sickness. We won't let it keep those of us who are well from finding our fortune." The man sat and grabbed the reigns, "Let us be off."

We climbed into our wagons and fell in behind him.

I stepped through the snow, dragging the iron pot behind me. It felt lighter. Maybe I was getting stronger. Maybe going where gold littered the streets would turn out well after all. If I could find gold, I could get money to go back to my family.

I wasn't as enthusiastic the next night. It had been a trying day. Mr. and Mrs. Miller had argued all afternoon, the wind had blown incessantly, and my arms ached from carrying the pot.

The wagon train stopped for the night and Mrs. Miller was getting dinner started. She shoved a bowl of shriveled potatoes at me, "Peel and dice these, Miriam."

"Yes, Mother." The response was automatic to me.

I took the bowl, and sat on a fallen tree near the fire. I felt so strange, so cold. My eyes could barely focus. What was happening to me?

I concentrated on the knife in the bowl. I reached and grabbed hold of its handle. The world swirled around me. Am I dying? I wondered suddenly. Is this how it feels to die? Is this how Aunt Matilda felt?

The knife slipped out of my fingers and the bowl fell from my lap. My limbs were of no use. I would never see my family again. As the world grew dark, all I could think of was dying in that place . . .

June

I watched as Meg bounded through the snow, like the deer we'd seen playing behind the house that morning. Ten years old, and so full of life! She ran to me, "June, do you think your baby will be a boy or a girl?"

"I don't know," I laughed. "What do you think?"

We continued our walk, and I watched her young face as she thought.

Finally she said, "I think I can't guess." She looked up at me, "But that's part of the fun, isn't it? Not knowing what it will be."

"I suppose it is."

She slipped her hand in mine. It was small and warm, "And we'll love it no matter what."

I smiled down at her, "Yes we will. No matter what."

Meg kept my hand as we continued to walk. Yes, I would love my baby, no matter what.

Lilly

I had fallen in the snow; but no, I was in a bed. I was sitting atop Shandra, up in the mountains. How long had I been away from the cottage? It felt so long. Aunt Matilda would be cross. Supper was probably ready. She would be waiting for me.

My whole body ached. I could hear voices, far away and indistinct.

Someone was shouting, "Mr. Miller, let me and my wife take her until she's well."

Mr. Miller's voice boomed, echoing inside my head, "No! She's mine!" I wanted to escape, cover my ears; but I couldn't move, couldn't tell where my arms were. "You can't take her, Mr. Duckson, ever!"

The sound was lost. All was lost. Was it a moment? An hour? A day?

"Karl, the girl can't eat. She'll die soon, and then what good will she be?" Mrs. Miller whined. "Let the Ducksons deal with her. I haven't any taste for a corpse in my wagon."

What was she talking about? I felt fine, or did I? Where was I?

Mr. Miller replied harshly, "Are you going soft on me, Emmy?"

She was offended, "I've never been soft in my life!" She huffed, "All I'm saying is, if there's someone who will to take her off our hands before she dies, and causes us more bother, we ought to let them!"

"I think you're crazy Emmy, but..."

The voice faded into silence again. I was somewhere between waking and sleeping, a place I'd never been. I felt like I was sinking, my mind searching for something to grasp. It settled on one thought as the darkness grew deeper. I was the one who was dying.

June

The sun sank into the horizon once again. The sky was a pale blue where it met the trees in the distance. I turned back inside the house and sat down in front of the fireplace. Joshua was the only one home that evening; the others had gone sledding with Jacob.

Joshua looked up from the figure he'd been whittling the last three days.

I smiled, "What have you been working on?"

He smiled back, "Just a little thing. Have you thought of any names for the baby yet?"

I looked down at the bump that had been plainly visible the last weeks, "I'm not sure. There are so many nice names."

He nodded, "There are a lot."

The conversation lulled for a minute. The only sounds were that of knife against wood and burning logs. He turned to the window, "The others have been out for some time. Do you think they'll be getting back soon?"

"Yes, soon."

My mind went back to December. That beautiful day we'd shown Lilly how to sled. How innocent she was when she first came out of the mountains, never having seen anyone besides her aunt. She'd only been gone for three months, but it felt much longer. I wished she would be there when the baby came. She would have loved to help pick a name.

Lilly

Something warm was in my mouth. I swallowed. The hot liquid warmed me all the way down my throat.

A woman spoke near me, "She swallowed. Frank, she swallowed!"

A man's voice answered her in a low whisper, "Give it to her slowly, Harriet. She's been laid up a long time."

I felt a spoon being pressed to my lips again. The warm liquid dripped into my mouth. It rolled down my throat too quickly, and I coughed. The coughing racked my entire body. Someone slid an arm under my neck and lifted my head so I could swallow, and then my head was laid back on a soft pillow. Peace washed over me as I fell back into my endless night.

I was roused from my sleep at times. A gentle hand on my forehead, a few drops of broth, a warm cloth washing my face and arms. Sleep became a blessing and a comfort instead of the torture it had been before.

One day, a different hand lifted my head from the pillow. A large, calloused hand. The voice I heard was just as large and warm as the touch, "I'll do what I can. She's pretty far gone. She may not . . ."

There were sounds all around me. They seemed far away from where I lay. Someone was close. Who was it; Mr. Miller? No, the presence was too still.

I was awake, but my eyes remained shut. I tried to open them, but they wouldn't. I saw a faint glow of light. I felt as though I hadn't stirred in months. I wanted to lift my hand to touch my closed eyelids, but only my fingers moved. How strange I felt.

Someone came near, then was still. I wondered who it was.

I concentrated on opening my eyes, and finally they did open, slowly and narrowly. Light blinded me, and for a moment it was all I could see. Then it dimmed, and a man came into focus, looking down at me. It wasn't Mr. Miller, or anyone else from the wagon train. He was familiar though. He had looked down on me like this before, sometime long ago.

He knelt beside the mattress I was lying on. The man put his hand on my forehead and waited, then smiled almost imperceptibly. His eyes looked steadily into my own, "Lilly, I'm Judge Harris."

Of course! I remembered him; but if I was with him, was I home? My eyes darted around the space we were in. It was the back of a wagon, but not the Millers'.

My lips parted, but all that came out was a small croak. The judge must have seen my confusion, "You're still on the wagon train. Do you remember what happened, Lilly?"

I couldn't remember. Had I been sleeping?

"It's alright," he said, "You don't have to talk right now. I'll get you some water."

He left and brought back a mug and spoon. I blinked heavily and let my eyes close again while I took a spoon full of the warmed water and swallowed it.

I awoke again sometime later. This time my eyes opened easily.

Judge Harris was still there and placed a large hand on my forehead. He looked relieved, but tired. He had a bowl of broth in his hand. He filled the small spoon, put it to my lips, and let warm liquid fall into my mouth. I swallowed it easier than I had before. It was soothing to my dry throat.

After two more spoons he set the bowl down, "Lilly, you've been very ill," he said gently, "But you're going to get better now."

"Judge Harris?" My voice was only a whisper.

He tucked the quilt back up to my chin, "Go to sleep now. We'll talk in the morning."

He jumped down from the wagon, and I felt a light breeze as the canvas fell back. I closed my eyes again. It felt so good to be awake and know what was happening around me. To talk to someone. For so long, I only had the Millers; but now the judge would help me, and I would see my family again.

The next morning Judge Harris came in soon after I awoke. I had been listening to the sounds of the camp and the birds singing.

The judge knelt down and felt my forehead again. He seemed pleased, "You got through it, Miss Lilly."

I took a deep breath before speaking. My voice was not as rough as it had been the night before, "Where are we, Judge?"

"I'm a doctor here," he answered, "You're still on the wagon train, but you're in the Ducksons' wagon. The Millers don't know I'm here. They gave you to Mr. and Mrs. Duckson two weeks ago."

The Ducksons had been taking care of me? The Millers must not have wanted to deal with my illness. "How did you get here?" I asked.

"I was a doctor before I became a judge. The wagon trains have been struck hard with the Rocky Mountain fever lately, so I came to help." He hesitated a moment, "Do you . . ."

He paused before going on, "When you get stronger, I'll take you home. I want you to sit up and sip some broth."

He folded a thick quilt, and gently lifted me to put it under my shoulders. I tried to help him by leaning up myself, but I couldn't. He saw me struggling, and frowned as he lowered me back onto the blanket.

When I was settled, he said, "Can you lift your arm for me?"

Without thinking I tried to lift one arm. It

felt like a heavy weight lay on it. I strained and pulled. Finally, my arm hung several inches above the mattress. My eyes were on the Judge's darkened expression. When I couldn't hold it any longer I let it drop beside me. My breath came heavily.

He gave me a moment before turning to pick up the bowl of broth he had brought in. He gave it to me slowly, each spoonful only holding a few drops. When I looked up, he avoided my eyes. He just watched the spoon as he brought it to my mouth and back to the bowl.

June

"Margret, would you come and finish setting the table for me?"

A moment later Margret bounced into the kitchen and took the plates out of my hands. She smiled as she set them out and got the forks, "Meg is amazing! She's reading Pilgrim's Progress already!" She nodded toward the door, "Take a peak."

I smiled and stirred the pot of beans once more before stepping into the doorway. Jacob and Joshua sat facing Meg, listening intently. Meg's young voice deepened or softened according to the character she was reading for. The story seemed to take on a life of its own in our small home.

When the chapter ended she looked up to where I stood by the kitchen door.

I smiled, "That was beautiful, Meg! Mr. Bunyan should have heard you read his work."

She closed her book and hugged it tightly against her chest, too ecstatic to speak.

Margret came and wrapped her arm around my shoulders, "Come on, everybody. Supper's ready."

When the dishes were cleared, and we were all sitting around the table, I gave Jacob a secret *look. He turned to Meg, "We have something for you, Meg."*

Her eyes quickly filled with wonder, "You do?"

Jacob nodded.

I went over to the cupboard and pulled out a small birthday cake. The second I turned back to the table everyone yelled, "Happy Birthday!"

Meg clasped her hands, "I almost forgot! My birthday! And you made a cake."

We split the cake into five equal pieces. I suggested we split it into six and that I get two, one for me and one for the baby. That idea was rejected, but when none of the others were looking, Jacob slipped me a bit of his piece.

I quickly put it in my mouth; and when the others turned back, my cheeks were full of cake.

Margret sucked in her breath, "Oh!"

Joshua looked puzzled and Meg started laughing, "You snuck her more cake!"

Lilly

I slipped in and out of sleep the entire day. Each time I woke, Judge Harris was at my side, watching, waiting, always ready with a bowl of warm broth to feed me.

At last, I woke up and knew it was a new day. The light was still faint and only a few birds were singing. Judge Harris was sleeping on the wagon floor, but stirred when I coughed.

His eyes were tired, but he tried to smile, "Good morning, Lilly. You slept the whole night through."

I didn't try to speak; I only smiled.

He picked up the bowl of broth, "Are you ready for breakfast now?"

I nodded, and he sat me up like he had before. I ate several spoons full before he set the bowl aside, "Would you like to lie back down now?"

"Not yet," I said quietly.

Several minutes later I asked, "Is the train still moving?"

"It has been off and on, but not at all for the last two days. They'll be starting again in a couple of hours."

"Are we going home?"

"We'll have to continue with the wagon train until you've regained your strength. Then we'll get you home."

"Won't the Millers want me back?" I asked.

"We're going to pretend you're still sick. They gave you to the Ducksons because they thought you would pass soon. As long as they think you're sick, they'll stay away. They don't want any trouble."

I put my head back on the pillow. I was safe, and would soon be reunited with my family.

A few days later, I felt like I could sit up more to have my breakfast. Judge Harris slipped several blankets under my back. When he sat back down and picked up the bowl and spoon, I noticed he had his coat off and his shirt sleeves were rolled up to the elbows. Thinking about it, I realized I was warm too. Ever since I got sick, I'd been covered in a heavy quilt.

"Could I take the covers off? I'm a little warm," I said.

He studied my face, "Lilly, you lost a lot of weight during these past four weeks. You may have trouble regulating your body temperature." He stopped, "I suppose if you're warm, it would be alright."

He folded back the covers for me. I felt so free with the quilt off, almost like I could get up.

I looked down at myself. I was dressed in what must have been Mrs. Duckson's nightgown, but I didn't recognize myself. I could see how thin my legs were beneath the fabric. My arms and wrists looked too weak to even lift my bony hands. I had always been small, but never in poor health. I wondered how my face must look.

I looked up at the doctor's face. He could see my concern, "You'll be alright. You'll be as strong as ever."

A tear rolled down my cheek. I would have brushed it away, but I felt like it would have been impossible to lift my hand that far. The doctor dried it with his handkerchief, as his own tears started to fall.

Why was he crying with me? I wanted to ask him. I wanted to know what was making him sad. I searched his face for an explanation he wasn't going to give.

He wiped away his own tear and gave me a moment, "Would you like the broth now?"

I nodded. I didn't want breakfast anymore, but I knew I had to eat.

A week later Judge Harris climbed into the wagon to bring me breakfast.

I felt good that day, "Good morning, Doctor."

"Good morning, Lilly."

As he moved the chair closer, I pulled my hand out from under the quilt and brushed a curl from my face. When I had laid my arm down at my side, I realized what I had done! I looked at the doctor's startled expression. I hadn't lifted my hand that far since being ill. He looked from my face and down to my thin arm. I looked at it too. Could I do it again? I watched my fingers as I told them to move, lift, and come near my face again.

They lifted and again pushed a stray curl back from my forehead. I lowered my arm slowly, and dropped it to the bed. Elation spread through me, my limbs warming with the knowledge that I was getting better.

Three more times that day, Doctor Harris had me raise and lower each arm.

That evening, he asked if it would be alright if the Ducksons came in to see me. I suddenly wanted very much to see them. I had forgotten I was in their wagon!

"Where have they been staying this whole time?" I asked.

"When they took you in they moved what they needed outside. Mr. and Mrs. Duckson took good care of you, but they were careful not to catch the fever themselves, and wouldn't let Cody see you no matter how much he begged."

"I would like to see them, if it's alright," I said.

He went out and, a moment later, the canvas was pulled back again.

Cody jumped up into the wagon, and his parents came after him. As soon as he saw me awake, he ran to me and wrapped his arms around my neck. I'd rarely been hugged, but it was comforting to be loved and cared for.

"Lilly, you slept for so long!"

I wrapped my arms around him. Tears ran down my cheeks, "I know, but I'm better now," I whispered.

I smiled as Cody let go of my neck. Mrs. Duckson bent over and stroked my hair back, "It's good to see you better, Lilly."

Mr. Duckson nodded.

After several minutes of visiting, Mr. Duckson said to his son, "We better let Lilly rest now." He turned to me, "We'll see you in the morning."

"Thank you," Tears rolled down my cheeks again, "Thank you so much."

Mrs. Duckson knelt on the floor and held my hand, "Good night, Lilly." She studied my face, then hugged me again and whispered in my ear, "I knew you'd get better."

They left the wagon, and it was quiet again.

Could she love me like a daughter? I'd never felt the feeling I did when Mrs. Duckson hugged me and whispered in my ear. I'd never had a mother. Many had cared for me; Aunt Matilda, Jacob, June, Joshua, Margret, Meg, and then this family. They took me in when I was sick, when I could have endangered their family with illness. They had taken care of a dying girl they barely knew.

Judge Harris climbed back into the wagon. He smiled slightly, "Are you ready for supper now?"

I had forgotten all about it, "Yes," I answered absent-mindedly, "I'm ready."

He sat down, and held the bowl close to me, "Try doing it yourself."

I looked down at the broth in the bowl.

Twenty minutes later I sipped the last spoonful and set it down in the empty bowl. I could see that the doctor was pleased, even though a smile never broke. The next sentence I spoke surprised me. I was looking into his dark eyes, "Are you happy, Doctor?"

Grave, steady eyes looked back at me, "I'm as happy as I can be."

There was more. I waited.

An eyebrow raised, "You're becoming a very perceptive young woman." He paused and settled back to tell a story, "Years ago I traveled hundreds of miles to places where there were no doctors. I had a wife and a little girl I left for months at a time to make those trips." A corner of his mouth curved up, "My wife, Delilah, was the kindest, most beautiful woman who ever lived. She was caring and independent," he sighed, "and stubborn. She wanted me to help those people just as much as I did." Tears came to his eyes, "It was just like any other trip. I hugged my wife, and kissed my little girl. I watched her bouncing, brown curls as I rode away." He was silent for a moment and then continued, "I returned two months later to find my Delilah gone and my daughter ill with the same thing that had taken my wife. Neighbors had done all they could to help. I sat with her for hours, but I was too late."

He closed his eyes gently. I looked down to his hand resting on the mattress, and put my own hand over it, "I'm sorry."

His eyes opened. They were full of pain,

"There's more, Lilly."

I waited, wondering what more there could be.

"The next year, I went on another trip. I had to get away. As I was coming back over the hills, I came to a grassy clearing with an old cottage and a frantic woman who didn't know how to care for the ailing young girl who lived with her. I tended to the girl for over a week before her health returned. She was a lively little one with a slight frame, sparkling clear eyes with long lashes that brushed her cheeks when she blinked, and shining brown curls." The doctor bowed his head, "She was the same age as my little girl."

He stopped, his eyes full.

"What happened?" I whispered.

He raised his head, the tears that had filled his eyes were overflowing now, "She reminded me so much of my little one . . . I couldn't leave her. I asked the woman if I could stay a little longer to ensure the girl's health had fully returned. She told me I could, and I stayed for two more weeks." His look was distant, "Those were the happiest days I had spent since losing my wife and daughter. The little girl called me her friend. Those bright eyes looked up into my own with such trust and hope. She brought me bouquets of lilies and wild flowers and took my hand in her own as we walked through the woods."

"Then the woman told me it was time to go." The light in his eyes suddenly faded, "They had been alone in the hills for a long time. I tried to tell her she'd be better off coming to town." His head bowed, "She wouldn't be convinced. She seemed afraid. She told me to leave and never come back. I didn't have a choice. She went inside the little house, got my bags and walked me to the edge of the clearing."

The doctor's grey eyes were so dark, so pained, "I looked back on the little girl playing by the cabin. She had given life back to me. I listened to her bright laughter for the last time as I walked away."

He looked into my eyes, "The little girl who lived in the hills with her Aunt Matilda was named Lilly."

Suddenly I stiffened beneath the doctor's tender gaze. He knew me when I was a little girl. He knew me when I'd been old enough to run and laugh, but not old enough to remember seeing his face and hearing his voice. Yet there was something about him that put me at ease the first morning we met.

He had probably saved my life when I was a child, and now he had done it again. "Thank you," I said softly.

He looked startled, "For what?"

"For taking care of me then, and now. And for loving me," tears were streaming down my cheeks, "like a daughter."

June

My hand was warm in Jacob's as we walked down the road, and the air was no longer cold. Spring had come. I hadn't noticed until there were suddenly birds and flowers everywhere I looked.

And it would be time to till the garden soon. The same thought must have been running through Jacob's mind as well, "What do you want to plant in the garden this year?" he asked.

"I don't think I'll be able to decide," I answered quickly, "I want to plant everything!"

He smiled, "I know what you mean. It feels like it's been such a long winter. But," he looked up at the intense, blue sky, "it's over now."

Our walk took us through town and then home again.

Meg skipped to us as we walked in the door, "See what Margret taught me in arithmetic?"

She triumphantly displayed her slate with an equation written on it, and explained how it was done. She was a quick and eager student, and Margret was a patient and creative teacher. Anything she explained was immediately soaked up by her young pupil. Margret had also been working to teach Joshua all the things he'd missed by not being in school.

With much of the teaching being done by Margret, the cooking by her and Meg, and the outdoor chores by Joshua, I was free to help where I wanted and prepare for the baby. I spent many happy hours sewing baby clothes.

Only four months and my baby would be here.

Lilly

After giving me a bowl of broth the next afternoon, Judge Harris looked down at me, contemplating for a moment, "I have to go for a while, Lilly. Other wagon trains have the fever and need a doctor."

His eyes were sad. I wanted to comfort him, "You'll do a lot of good for them." I said, "When will you go?"

"This evening." He paused, "I don't want to leave you. I stayed this long because I had to know you were well. I feel as though you could be my own daughter." He quickly wiped away a tear, "I don't want to leave you."

I didn't know what to say. I didn't want him to go either. I felt safe with him and wanted him to take me home.

He spoke again, "I've told the Ducksons to pretend you're still sick, so the Millers will leave you alone. They'll take good care of you while I'm gone." He wiped away another tear, "Keep eating your broth."

I nodded. He turned, climbed out of the wagon, and was gone. I lay still, thinking. I felt numb. I felt like I had lost my only way to get home.

A little while after he had left, Mrs. Duckson stooped beneath the wagon cover and looked down at the untouched bowl of broth beside me. She picked it up, left, and returned with a fresh dish.

She sat on the edge of the mattress and fed me, one spoonful at a time. It was the first time in days I hadn't fed myself. We didn't speak as I ate. I didn't feel, yet I felt everything. Every emotion lay inside of me. I swallowed the broth I was given, and let my mind stop thinking.

Over the next few days Mrs. Duckson sat at my bedside while I ate. I slowly started feeling stronger again. I missed the doctor, but Mrs. Duckson was kind. I wanted to be able to smile when she sat next to me.

A week after the doctor left, Cody came in the wagon holding a bowl, "I brought you supper. Mother mashed meat and potatoes in it tonight."

I took the bowl, smiled at him, and he left the wagon happily.

When I finished, I felt more satisfied. I started eating more and more solid foods. At night, the family gathered in the wagon to eat supper and to talk. I loved them. Cody's sparkling eyes and ready smile, Mr. Duckson's gentle ways, and Mrs. Duckson's love and consistency. They asked me to call them Frank and Harriet. We grew closer every day.

I started being able to pull myself up on my own while pillows were put behind my back and I could stay awake for most of the day.

One afternoon, two weeks after the doctor had left, Harriet climbed into the back of the wagon. She smiled, "Lilly," She placed her hands on her hips, "I think you can get up now."

I nodded, even with my doubts, "I'll try. Will you help me?"

"Of course!"

I was already sitting up. Harriet watched as I moved one leg, then the other to bring myself to the edge of the bed. It was the first time I'd sat up with nothing behind me. It wasn't as hard as I thought it would be. She helped me to stand and held both my hands as I took one step, then two, then three.

For several more days, I walked back and forth in the wagon bed, always with someone holding my hand, smiling, and encouraging me.

On the sixth day, Frank climbed hurriedly into the back of the wagon, "The Millers have taken off ahead of the wagon train," he breathed. "Apparently, it was taking too long for them. They're gone!" He smiled down at me, "That means you can go outside."

I was free! "Can I go out right now?" I asked.

"I don't see why not."

With Cody and Frank's help I was able to get down from the wagon bed. As soon as my feet touched the earth, I felt alive again. Each sweet breath was filled with the memories of summer, and the smell of grass and trees was so much like it had been in the mountains. So much like home.

But there was something new in the air. The smell of dirt; and the wind was not as heavy as in the mountains.

I looked around. A horse kicked up dust walking across camp. The trees were few and far between, and unlike any I'd seen before. The grass broke beneath my feet instead of bending and springing back toward the sky when I stepped away.

I turned to the Ducksons, "What happened to the earth?"

They burst into laughter. Cody finally answered, "It's dry when you go west!"

"Oh," I laughed with them. It was hard to believe oxen could take us somewhere so different from where we were before.

June

I poked at the earth around a short, leafy tomato plant stalk. The ground was moist, but a little more watering wouldn't hurt it. I straightened slowly. It was growing ever more strenuous getting things done. The baby would come any time now.

Many women were dizzy with worry by this point, but I wasn't.

I felt a little nervous but ready to have my little one. I wondered again if it would be a boy or a girl. Sometimes I wondered what he or she would look like. Would they have Jacob's steady gaze and square jaw, or my slight frame and wavy hair?

I looked at the young, stalky tomato plant. I knew what it would be when it had fully matured, and how to best care for it and help it become all that it could. Would I know how to care for my little one, to help them become all they wished to become?

I put my hands against the small of my back and winced at the pain. I stretched, trying to relieve it. Nothing seemed to help anymore.

I turned my face to the blue sky and blazing sun. I could almost feel the beads of sweat evaporating in the intense July heat. I looked back to the young tomato plant as the pain rose again. I winced, wishing Doctor Harris would return. I wanted him there when the baby came.

Lilly

I put my foot down in the dusty brown grass. The first time I'd set my foot in the dry weeds of the prairie was only two months before, when I had recovered enough to walk. Since then, I'd taken many steps farther west each day of our journey.

I had walked nearly a mile that day with Cody beside me. "Lilly, do you know where we'll get to tomorrow?" he asked.

"Where?"

"Bent's Old Fort. Everybody knows about it!" He said excitedly, "We'll buy our food and water there, and meet all sorts of people. Some of them might join our train."

I looked ahead. It was hard to believe something besides grass and dirt and more hills lay beyond the horizon.

"Is it very large?" I asked.

His eyes widened in disbelief, "Of course it's large! It's the biggest fort from here to the Pacific Ocean!"

My heart leaped inside of me. The Pacific Ocean! I'd only heard of it from the talk around camp. I tried to imagine the water stretching to the horizon, and beyond.

The next day we could see the Rocky Mountains in the distance long before we saw the fort; but by afternoon, its walls could be seen against the sky and jutting hills.

We walked through its tall dust-blown, wooden doors an hour later. I'd never seen walls made like that. Cody told me they were called adobe. He couldn't contain himself. He pointed out fur traders, a flag blowing in the wind, an enormous press in the center of the fort, and everything else he had time to say the name of before he saw the next thing.

I could hardly hear his explanations while trying to take in everything around me. It was the densest crowd of people I'd ever seen. Some were white like myself and all the other people I'd met, but many had dark brown skin.

I leaned close to Cody's ear, and pointed to one brown-skinned man, "His skin isn't like ours."

He didn't seem surprised, "He's an Indian."

I looked at the man again, and looked away, still confused. Cody only lifted an eyebrow and looked at me for a moment before turning his attention to his mother.

The only reason for entering the fort that night was to appease our growing curiosity about it. After walking through it, we went back to our wagon that was sitting in line with the rest of the train.

The sounds coming from inside the fort didn't subside with the setting of the sun. We lay awake in our wagon far into the night, listening to the mix of tongues and lowing of oxen.

Cody woke us, and possibly the whole camp, the next morning. He fidgeted all during breakfast until his father finally said it was time to go in again. The mass of people was just as dense as it had been the night before. Frank took us to various traders whose wares were carefully arranged. He bought food and barrels of water.

We carried our goods with us as we went from one trader to another, examining their things. After a while, we went back to our wagon to put the supplies away. It felt strange to sit idle in the middle of the day, but there wasn't anything to do except wait while Frank went back in to trade the furs they'd brought with them.

After all the trading was done, it was finally time for our company to move out. Many other wagons joined our train. The fort disappeared in a cloud of dust, as we turned our attention to the mountains ahead.

June

I let my breath out as the pain eased and wiped the perspiration from my face. Jacob walked back into the bedroom with a mug of water and held it to my lips. I took a small sip before lying back on the stack of pillows. It soon started again: a terrible, clenching pain. In a few moments, it subsided again.

Lilly

One week after leaving Bent's Old Fort, we were deep into the crests and valleys that had appeared so insignificant in the distance. What had only been mounds of dirt were each an entire day's journey to cross.

As we came to the crest of one such hill, I turned to look over the valley we had crossed. Well behind us, I could see the young couple's wagon, struggling to move up the steep slope. Frank, who had walked and let Cody ride that day, seemed to notice it at the same moment I did.

He called to Harriet, who was driving the oxen, "They're having trouble behind us. Stop the wagon. We'll go back to help."

Immediately, the wagon stopped and Cody and Harriet jumped down. They took one look at the struggling oxen and started back down to help them. I followed. I wanted to help, but I was exhausted from our climb and from the heat of the day.

Rocks slid and shifted beneath our feet. I looked for solid places to step, but there weren't many.

My foot slid onto its side and got wedged between the rocks time and again. I set my foot down again and winced in pain. That foot would be bruised and swollen for days.

June

I tried to relax as the pain eased; and I rested my eyes, trying to sleep for a few precious moments, but I heard the front door opening and Margret speaking to someone. She walked in with the midwife.

Jacob looked relieved, "I'm so glad you're here."

She quickly rolled up her sleeves and washed her hands in the basin before coming to the bedside, "Keep hot water ready and get clean towels."

Jacob left and the midwife bent over me. She held my wrist to take my pulse and rubbed a cloth across my damp forehead.

The pain was coming back. I didn't think I could do it again.

I took her hand in mine and squeezed hard.

Lilly

We stood on either side of the young couple's wagon. They sat on the buggy seat, the woman holding her young baby while we held on, pulling alongside their oxen. I tried not to pay attention to my shoes being shredded by the rocks as we climbed.

Once we pulled the wagon out of the rut it was in, we kept walking with the oxen until it pulled up behind our own wagon.

I looked back down the hill we'd climbed twice, and then ahead, where the rest of the train was struggling. After a few yards of even ground another slope began. I lifted my skirt to look down at my shoes. They would be gone soon.

June

"*I need to push!*" *I shouted as the midwife checked the baby's position.*

Jacob came over to hold my hand, "You can do it! The baby will be here before you know it." When the next pain came, I started pushing as I held onto Jacob's strong hand, "Keep going, June. You're doing great!"

Lilly

We made camp at the top of one of the slopes that night. Everyone's shoes had been shredded. Many of the others had spare shoes, but our family didn't. We sat in a circle around the fire, rubbing our feet, and propping them up to help relieve the swelling.

"What will we do for shoes now?" Cody asked.

Frank reached over and tousled Cody's light hair, "We'll tie cloth around our feet. It'll be even more comfortable than our old shoes." He smiled and Cody laughed.

Mr. Duckson was always lighthearted and helped us stand up to the hard days. We would smile no matter how hard the journey grew.

We lay in the wagon that night, completely exhausted. The mountainside was quiet. The next day we would scale an even more daunting slope.

June

The midwife stood at the foot of my bed with Jacob next to her, holding a small bundle of blankets. A wail burst from the bundle and a little hand reached up toward Jacob's smiling face.

He looked up, brought the bundle to me and placed it gently in my arms.

I looked into Jacob's eyes. He smiled again, and caressed the crown of our baby's soft head, "It's a girl," he whispered.

I looked back down at her little face. The dark brown hair, blue eyes, and small nose. She looked just like me. And Lilly.

"Jacob, let's call her Miriam," I said quietly.

He looked from her small face to mine. His eyes seemed to be full of love and pure joy, "That's a beautiful name," he said softly.

Lilly

For a week more, we climbed the crumbling side of the mountain. By the end of that week, more people had come down with the fever. Everyone was afraid of contracting it; we knew how much sorrow it brought. Some lay in their wagons with no one caring for them as we made our way out of the mountains. They had come so far only to die within weeks of reaching their destination.

My family wouldn't rest while anyone was in need. At every stop, we would go through the camp, taking hours to feed the recovering and soothe the mourning. My heart broke along with each heart that was stilled. I couldn't look at them, couldn't help in their burial.

Frank and Harriet became too worn down, and two days out from the Rocky Mountains, after watching so many die, Cody and I stood helplessly by as they both passed on.

Late into the night, Cody and I sat beside their graves. If only Judge Harris had been there, he might have saved them. I had done everything I could think of. They had only wanted to help others and ended up giving their lives for them. They kept Cody and me at a distance whenever they thought someone was contagious, but had gone in fearlessly themselves.

Our wagon lay behind us in the camp. The night was dark and still, like so many other nights.

The ground was dusty and warm; the sky was velvety black and studded with stars. I felt like the world could not go on when they weren't there to take us forward. Could Cody and I make it alone?

I looked down at Cody's tear-streaked face. I had to take care of him. He had laid his head down in my lap and cried himself to sleep. I would get him the rest of the way to California; to his aunt and uncle.

I lay down on the ground beside Cody and put my arm around him. We would be a family now; we would make it together. When the sun rose the next morning, we got in our wagon seat and followed the trail west.

That night, a scream woke me. I sat up quickly. There had been screaming in my dreams, but it was real; it woke me up. I wondered if whoever had screamed needed help. Frank and Harriet would have answered the cry, but I was so tired. I didn't want to see any more despair or heartache.

I took a breath. It didn't matter how hard it might be, I had to help. Tears filled my eyes as I rewrapped my feet in the old rags I used as shoes, and climbed out of the wagon without waking Cody. Someone else was probably dying of the fever. I didn't want to see the face of another dying man, woman, or child, or the sadness in the eyes of the ones they left behind.

I walked in the direction the sounds had come from. Everything was still as I passed the wagon closest to ours.

As I came to the second wagon, the one that belonged to the young couple, I heard their infant crying. I stood still for a moment, listening to the baby. That must have been what I had heard. I turned back, then stopped. The infant continued to wail, but I knew it wasn't the sound I heard before. I was sure I had heard something like an animal.

I looked around in the darkness. I wanted to run back to our wagon and bury myself under the covers, but I had to check on them.

I turned back to the wagon and walked cautiously to the loose canvas flap. The wind blew it aside enough for me to look in.

The place was a mess. Everything inside had been scattered, and in a far corner lay an overturned cradle. Buried in the tangle of blankets, behind the cradle rails, squirmed the young couple's two-month old infant. The man and his wife were gone.

A sound in the grass behind me made me jump. I clambered into the wagon, and looked around. My hands shook as I saw deep, bloody scratches covering the floor around the cradle.

I lifted the cradle and picked up the small bundle. The little one quieted as soon as I climbed down from the wagon and pulled it close. I hurried back to our wagon. I wanted to get someone to look for her parents then, but the wolf could still be around the camp.

I rewrapped the baby and laid her between Cody and myself. She was so small and still; and as I listened to her steady breathing, my own breathing calmed a little.

The next morning, a search party went out to look for her parents. The man who led our wagon train came to me when the party returned. His face was downcast, "We found them."

I swallowed before asking, "Are they ---"

"Yes," he interrupted then looked down at the little baby I held, "She'll need someone to take care of her."

I nodded, "I know."

June

She was my own little baby. Margret, Meg, Joshua, and Lilly; we'd been a family since the day we all came together, but my own blood ran through this little one.

I looked down on Miriam in her cradle, already two weeks old, my sweet, sleeping little bundle.

Lilly

I turned back to the trail from watching the baby. We'd had her for two days, but no one in the wagon train seemed to take much notice.

Cody held and cuddled her as long as she wanted. I hadn't been sure of what to feed her at first. I eventually decided to boil our dinner before eating it and feed her the water from it. Our food was flavorless, but the baby seemed happy.

Cody, who had been walking, ran up beside the oxen, "Lilly, what day was the baby born?"

I thought for a moment. I remembered a sunny day in April when the announcement spread through the train that the young couple's baby had been born, "I think it was April sixth."

Cody laughed in merriment, "That's a good birthday. I like April!"

I smiled at the mention of birthdays, "Cody," I said, "Tomorrow is June twenty-third. That's my birthday!"

He grinned and skipped a couple of times, "I love birthdays! Let's have a party."

We had our celebration the next night. After our dinner of boiled jerky and rice, we sang all the songs either of us knew, and the baby and I watched Cody dance around the fire until he was worn out. Then we both sat and rested by the fire.

I sat looking into the baby's bright eyes, "Cody, let's call the baby Clara," I said.

He nodded, "Clara. I like that name." A minute later he asked, "Lilly, how old are you today?"

"Seventeen," I answered.

Several minutes passed, and Cody fell asleep against my shoulder. I wrapped my arm tighter around little Clara and listened to Cody's slow breathing. A wolf howled in the distance. Everything else was silent.

I felt so different than I ever had before. This family, my family, was different than being with Jacob and June, Joshua, and Meg, or even when Frank and Harriet were still with us. This was my family; a family I was responsible for. It felt daunting, yet I looked forward to each day of leading and caring for them. Every time I thought of California, excitement ran through me.

Then I remembered Cody's uncle. He would be waiting for his brother and his family, but all he'd get was his nephew and a young girl with a baby in her arms, bearing news of his brother's passing.

What would he think of three young people coming to his home? Two of them, no relation to him.

Three more weeks of traveling brought us to the place where we would join other travelers on the California trail. No more epidemics had threatened us. The route had turned from rocky slopes to long, rolling plains.

The sky seemed to go on forever. I felt as if I could stand on my toes to peer over the next slope and see California lying ahead.

I loved the never-ending sky, vast plains, and constant wind that cooled us and our oxen.

I hadn't walked beside the wagon for nearly a month. I wanted to stay with Clara, but I couldn't stand the prospect of spending another day in that wagon seat.

After the breakfast dishes were done, I turned to Cody, "Can you take the first turn driving the wagon today?"

His eyes widened, "Really?"

I nodded, "Really! Do you think you can handle it?"

"Oh, yes! I think so."

"I'll carry Clara with me." I knelt down and took off her dirty diaper.

"I'll wrap an apron around us and tie her onto me." I finished pinning the new cloth onto Clara and picked her up, "Will you get me your mother's old apron, Cody?"

He ran to the wagon and got out the apron Harriet always wore. He walked back to me slowly, staring down at the familiar length of cloth.

When he got to me, I lay my hand on it. It was coarse and worn in spots from so many years of use. Suddenly I realized what seeing it must have done to him. The feel of it must have brought back memories of his childhood, of love. I left it in his hands, "I'm sorry, Cody. I wasn't thinking."

He shook his head, "No, she'd want you to use it."

I kissed his cheek and took the bundle from him. I held Clara close as I wound the cloth behind me, then back around us both, and tied it in front.

I slowly took my hands away and tugged here and there to make sure it was secure. I bounced up and down a couple of times. The apron held Clara in place, and she looked up at me from her little cocoon.

I stroked her soft, fuzzy head.

"Can we go now?" Cody asked eagerly.

I smiled and watched as everyone else got into their wagons, "Looks like it. Get to your seat!"

He bounced into the wagon seat and flicked the leather straps against the animals' backs, "Here we go!"

I laughed at his energy.

The day passed blissfully for our little family. Cody and I talked and laughed as he drove and I walked with Clara.

The scenery continued to send a thrill through every limb of my body. The sun, sky, grass, trees, hills and wind. All of it was beautiful and made me feel alive.

I loved to see Cody driving the wagon, looking like he'd been doing it all along. He mastered the oxen that first morning and smiled all afternoon. Clara loved the movement and closeness, and she was content all day long.

Several hours after dinner, another wagon train, miles long, stretched across the horizon. By supper we could smell their cooking fires.

I climbed in the buggy seat after dinner and sat next to Cody, "I'll ride while we join with the other wagon train. It might be a little crowded to walk."

His face tightened, "Maybe you should drive."

"Why's that?"

"I don't know if I can drive with all those other wagons around."

His eyes scanned the long line of wagons ahead. I put my arm around his shoulders. I hadn't noticed how tall he'd grown; his shoulders were nearly even with my own!

"Don't worry. You'll do just fine. Just keep aware of others, and I'll be right here when you need me."

Cody looked comforted and navigated the wagon with impressive precision. We were safely part of our new wagon train within the hour.

In another hour, we were through South Pass, and more mountains loomed ahead of us.

I hadn't expected to cross any more mountain ranges. I decided I wouldn't think about them then. All I would think of was living each day with my family, doing everything I needed to, and keeping the kids happy.

That night we formed circles with a dozen

wagons nearby. No one from our former wagon train was a part of our circle. We made and ate supper and went to bed without meeting each other. No one waited for anyone else the next morning. When a wagon was ready to head out, they joined with the others already moving along the trail.

When we finished breakfast, we merged into the line of wagons heading away from the rising sun and toward the still dark horizon.

We continued on the Oregon Trail for three more days before breaking onto the Lander Cutoff. The next stop would be Fort Hall, a place I'd never heard of before, but couldn't wait to come to. The Fort marked the place where we would rejoin the Oregon Trail.

The Lander Cutoff held an even bleaker landscape. The hills were no longer covered in long prairie grass. Instead, we looked out on a flat desert, stretching to the horizon.

Walking beside the wagon, I had to make my way through a maze of dense, dry bushes. The oxen trampled the brush in their path, as dust covered us and caught in our throats.

I had Clara tied onto me most of the time, which kept her from choking on the dust.

The sun beat down incessantly. It felt nearer than it had in the east. My skin was dark from its rays and chalky from the dust. Every time I untied the cloth from around Clara and brought her away from my body, the front of my dress was soaked in perspiration.

It was weeks before we saw Fort Hall's white walls in the distance. I didn't long for them anymore. What I longed for was the mountains and valleys of California, and for the comfort of Cody's uncle's home in the Sacramento Valley. I wanted to get there and never leave again. Then we could finally stop our endless march and be a family.

Fort Hall turned out to be nothing more than a fur-trading post. I didn't bother going inside. The place was crowded and wagons never stopped going in and out. We spent one night within sight of the fort and left the next morning.

That day at dinner I decided to give Clara something more than her usual broth. I over-boiled and then mashed some of the rice in my hands and mixed it with the broth until it made a milky liquid. She begged for more when it was gone.

I loved my little Clara more every day. She was starting to roll over whenever I set her down in the wagon bed at night. Her soft baby hair had grown and turned into a beautiful bright reddish-brown that shone in the sun.

Whenever she was without me, she would cry or look for me. I loved her, and so did Cody. I loved Cody too. I couldn't say how it happened. I'd never had a mother, but I was sure what I felt for both of them must have been a mother's love.

June

"Is my little girl two months old today?" Jacob held Miriam above his head. She smiled her sweet baby smile.

He put her on a blanket on the floor and sat down beside me. I leaned against him, "It seems like I just had her, but I don't know how I spent my time before."

Jacob nodded.

I let my head rest on his shoulder and closed my eyes, "I love her so much, Jacob."

He put his arm around me and brought me closer, "So do I. And I love you."

Meg and Margret came in from a walk, smiling and laughing, and sat down on the floor beside Miriam.

Jacob kissed me and stood, "I'm going out to help Joshua in the garden."

I smiled, "Alright. We'll have dinner ready when you two finish."

Lilly

We walked for another week and a half before leaving the Oregon trail and following the California trail. We followed the Raft River for a week, until it ended. Then we went on for another week before coming to the head of the Humbolt River.

As relieved as I was to see it, the Humbolt River was not as impressive as it had been in my imagination. In just a few days, the river turned to nothing more than an oozing trickle. The water began to smell and became unbearable to drink. The river never ran straight; it curved and switched back and forth with every mile. Sagebrush grew thick and sometimes stood well over our heads.

The river was lined with the carcasses of horses and oxen that had gone too far into the mire, and couldn't make it out. I was worried, not only for myself, but for Cody and Clara. The desert stretching to the horizon on either side of the trail was filled with coyotes that came to drink from the river. My breath froze every time I heard them in the night.

Another concern was the swarms of mosquitos borne of the foul water. The sun chased them away during the hottest part of the day, but there was no relief in the night. When we went to bed, we would tie the wagon cover down and buried ourselves in sheets, only to wake up in the morning with our faces itching and swollen.

To get water from the river, Cody and I had to find a place where there were no bushes or animal carcasses in the way, so we could step onto its banks and soak a blanket in the bitter water. We'd bring the dripping blanket back and wring it into our cooking pot. Nothing tasted good after boiling in that water.

After three weeks of following the hated Humbolt River, the dust we'd been breathing and eating and drinking had changed and began burning our skin and eyes.

We came to the edge of the Forty-Mile Desert nearly two weeks later. We filled everything we could with water. For the next four days, we would be crossing a barren wasteland with mountains on all sides. The sun glared off the white sand that surrounded us, and heat encompassed us as we prepared to take our first steps. Everyone stopped at its edge. Parents, children, and livestock looked out onto the desert.

The ground burnt my feet while the sun burnt my face, and Clara's body against my own only intensified the heat. Cody and I looked at each other; I took his hand in mine, and we started forward.

It was late in the afternoon. The sun finally sank below the horizon several hours later, but we didn't stop then. Night was when we had to cover the most ground. All I wanted was to sink into bed and let my body cool while I slept, but I couldn't.

All too soon, the sun rose behind us. Within minutes, the desert became an oven, intent on baking us.

We couldn't ever ride. The oxen were so thin that their ribs and shoulder blades poked out sharply beneath their skin.

We only stopped once that day to rest. By dinner time, the trail we were traveling was peppered with old wagons and rotting carcasses of oxen and horses. I could never stand the sight of any hurt or dying animal, and the smell was unbearable.

Walking through that burning desert, my mind turned back to when I was young.

Aunt Matilda and I had been walking through the trees, searching for herbs, when we came across a baby bird lying in the path.

I wanted to run back along the trail. I turned and buried my face in Auntie's skirt, tears running down my cheeks, "Oh, Auntie! The baby bird is sick. Make it better!"

She knelt down and held me away. Her face was stern and her sightless eyes were grave, "Lilly, you can't hide your face from things. If you see an animal that's hurt, you do what you can to help it; but if you can't, you face forward, and keep moving."

I no longer saw the animals to the side; but

Cody looked up at me, eyes overflowing with tears, "They're dead. Did anybody try to save them?" he whispered.

I stopped and put my hands on his shoulders. Tears filled my own eyes, seeing his pain and fear, "Cody, someone told me a long time ago that when you see pain or suffering, you do what you can to help; but if you can't, you face forward and keep moving."

I wiped the tears from his cheeks and gave him a hug, "These animals are already gone. Their suffering is over; but you, Clara, and I need to make it out of here with our oxen. We have a home waiting for us, Cody." I gave him a hug and whispered, "We'll make it there."

He nodded, new strength behind his eyes.

I looked down at Clara. My tears had fallen on her and run down her face; they seemed to cool her.

Cody and I took one resolute step after another until the following afternoon. It was during the hottest part of the day that I looked ahead and noticed people staring at a pile of debris as they slowly passed it by.

I hated to think what kind of mutilated scene lay there.

As we got closer, I saw it was a broken-down handcart filled with dust-covered belongings and empty food barrels.

In front of the cart, still holding the handle, were two men, one younger and one older, and a young woman. All of them were covered in dust, thin from lack of food, and listless. The older man and the girl lay completely still, but the younger man was moaning, rocking his head back and forth on the sandy earth.

No one had stopped to help them or even to see what they could do. The young man's eyes were swollen shut and his lips were cracked and covered in sand.

I didn't know what to do. What if I stopped? How could I help? I had my own family to watch over. I couldn't take on any more. Our food and water was running dangerously low already.

We passed by the people and their cart, but I looked back. Cody touched my arm, "Do you think we can do something?" he croaked.

I looked into his eyes, still filled with fear and red-rimmed, but with true compassion behind them.

"Yes," was all I could manage.

I grabbed the oxen's yoke, steered them to the side of the trail, and stopped several yards ahead of the cart. Wagons kept passing by. Most of the people never even turned to us but continued staring ahead, kicking up dust.

Clara was tied to me, "Cody, give the oxen just a taste of water, nothing more. And don't let any drip!"

He tended the oxen while I ran back with my canteen. I slowed as I came near, my heart pounding in my chest. The sight of the three dying figures made my stomach tighten. I wanted to turn and hide my face, but I couldn't. Not this time.

I was their last hope.

I went to the young man, who was still groaning. He lay beneath the handle of the handcart, probably where he'd dropped while pulling. He was broad-shouldered and had dark hair with the growth of several days on his jaw.

My throat tightened. I wanted to look away from his face, but I knew I couldn't. I had to do something.

I knelt on the burning ground, and a cloud of dust rose up around us. I took the cap off my canteen, held it against his lips, and let a few drops of water fall into his mouth. He coughed when the water reached his throat, then he swallowed it with difficulty.

When I took the canteen away I could see that the touch had drawn blood from his lips. I wiped the blood from the opening of my canteen and went to the older man.

It was too late. He was already gone.

When I came to the woman, the first thing I noticed was how beautiful she was. I saw past the dust that covered her and her red, swollen face. Her hair lay in long, soft blonde curls.

I was afraid she would be gone too, but her heart still beat faintly. I gave her a few drops of water, but she didn't respond. I don't even believe she swallowed. It simply soaked into her mouth.

When I finished, I went back to the wagon. Cody had just finished taking care of the oxen. His forehead creased when he saw me coming, "Lilly?"

I nodded, "We're going to stay here for a little while to help."

He smiled wearily. He knew staying meant someone was still alive.

"Let's bring the wagon closer," I said.

He climbed into the buggy and guided the oxen to where the people lay.

I wasn't sure how to move them so we left them where they were. Cody slept in the wagon bed, and I stayed up late into the night tending to the two young people.

Early the next morning, I found that the girl had slipped away sometime in the night.

When Cody woke, I told him we had to move the young man into the wagon, "We have to move on today. We'll be crossing the Sierras late as it is."

With much effort and straining, Cody and I were able to lift the man into the back of the wagon. When he was safely inside, there was nothing left to keep us in that spot. I hesitated to go on, leaving the two victims without even a burial.

Aunt Matilda's words came to my mind then, "When you can't help, face forward and keep moving."

I faced west, and with rags wrapped around my feet, I kept moving.

I was grateful when the two people and their handcart disappeared behind us and the only thing in sight was the endless desert. Because it was late in the year, no wagons came behind us. We were the last to cross, the last to attempt climbing the Sierra Nevadas for the year.

I went in and out of the wagon throughout the day. Each time letting water drip into the young man's parched mouth. I tried to wipe the dust off his face and he stirred slightly. I untied the rags from around his feet to help him cool off and left the wagon.

We rested during the hottest hours of the day and pressed forward straight through the night.

The sun shone on the mountains ahead when it rose the next morning. The Sierra Nevadas. We would finally come to the end of the desert. As soon as the thought came to me, I noticed how deep the sand beneath my feet had gotten. The wagon wheels dug further in, and the oxen's hooves sank deep with every step.

Early in the afternoon, the wagon stopped. I stood beside it for a moment before noticing and looking toward the oxen. They had stopped walking.

Cody and I silently grabbed onto either side of the wagon and pushed. After a while, I noticed that the sand had become more shallow. The wind stirred, and it was almost cool on my cheeks.

I looked up from the ground. There was a line of trees and bushes growing across the horizon. The oxen lifted their eyes to the same growth and suddenly started toward it. Water! They must smell water!

Two hours later we tripped through bushes and passed beneath leafy, shady, green cottonwood trees.

The oxen dashed into the water and dipped their heads in it.

I ran into the water. It was all around me, cool and clean. The Carson River! I knelt in it and drank as it flowed. I wet my face and arms and hair and dumped handfuls of it onto Clara who was still tied against me. Eventually, I thought of Cody. I looked up at the same moment he did. He had been doing the same thing.

We smiled at each other. We were alive! I pushed water at him and he splashed back, drinking life back into ourselves and laughing for the pure joy of living.

Part Three
Love

Lilly

Cody and I filled the canteens that hung around our necks and ran to the back of the wagon. We climbed in and while Cody started washing the young man's face I gave him a few more drops of water to drink.

He swallowed slowly then stirred, opened his eyes, and grabbed my hand. His grip was painful, "Adella!"

His raspy voice startled me, "Adella?" His eyes were dark, searching my face.

I suddenly felt frightened. I wondered what kind of a person I'd brought into my family's life. I pulled loose. The dirt that covered him had mixed with the water dripping off me and turned to mud on my wrist.

I reached for Cody, and he grabbed my hand. He seemed ecstatic at the young man's recovery, "He's alive, Lilly! He's going to live!"

I forced a smile, "Yes."

I looked back down. His eyes had taken on another look, one of bewilderment, "You're not Adella. Where's Adella, and my father?" He lifted his head, looked at Cody and back to me, and then to Clara strapped onto me, "Who are you?"

I opened my mouth, but couldn't get any

sound to come out. Cody answered quickly, "I'm Cody, and this is Lilly and Clara. We're a family." He said it proudly. I had never said anything of the sort out loud, but we all knew we were a family.

The man's eyes darted to me and back to Cody. Cody hadn't noticed my hesitation, but he had.

He addressed Cody, "I'm Will Haskim." His voice was less rough, "Where's my sister? And my father?"

Cody looked at me and then Will did too. I glanced down at Clara and took a deep breath. Then I looked back up and met his steady gaze, "Mr. Haskim, your father and sister are gone. They didn't make it."

Grief struck him instantly. His eyes grew darker and filled with tears, "I see."

"Is there anything we can do?" I whispered.

He looked lost, "Please, give me a moment."

I gave him my canteen and a piece of jerky before leaving the wagon.

I looked out onto the river, feeling there was a barrier between myself and the joy of the sun on the cool water.

June

Jacob came into the jailhouse with a playful smirk dancing across his face.

I leaned against the mop handle and placed my other hand on my hip, "What are you smiling about, Jacob Plyer?"

He shrugged, "I just met the man who bought the old house down the road from us."

He crossed the room and hung up his hat, still smiling, "His name is Elias. He just came from Missouri. He's a carpenter and he makes plows. He's very nice," he paused, "And single too. Margret might get along with him."

I laughed, "Jacob, you can't be serious! What do you know about him?"

Jacob shrugged, "I'm a lawman. I can tell about people, and I think he's a good one." He shrugged again and sat down behind the desk and started to sort through some papers, "Joshua and I could use some help building the new dinner table. A carpenter sure would come in handy."

"Fine," I dipped the mop in the bucket of water, "Just don't get your hopes up. I haven't seen any sign that Margret is looking for a husband."

Lilly

I untied the apron that was holding Clara against me. We were still dripping from our plunge into the river, "Cody, I'm going to bathe Clara and myself. You should too. You can go over there, beyond that bush hanging over the water, and I'll go the other way."

He started away; he seemed grateful for something to do with his energy. I was grateful for the diversion too, and more than ready to wash away all memories of the Forty-Mile Desert.

As we walked away from the wagon, I called to Cody, "Wash your clothes too."

"Alright," he called back and ran off.

I washed myself, Clara, and our clothes. Then I held Clara and let her splash in the water while we waited for our clothes to dry. I didn't have to wait long. Even at the water's edge, the air was incredibly dry.

After redressing and rewrapping the apron around Clara and myself, I ran my fingers through my hair and let it dry in the hot air.

It was refreshing to be clean!

I took a drink from the river and let Clara drink from my hand. As I came back to the wagon I could see a tall, lean man checking the oxen's legs. He turned when I came up behind him. His hair was darker after being washed, and he was even taller than I had thought before.

"Will Haskim?" I muttered.

He gave me a large, comfortable grin, "Yes," his voice was low and resonant, "Lilly?"

I nodded.

"Is there a last name that goes with that?"

"No. I mean, I don't . . ." I stopped, unable to decide what to say.

Cody came up behind me just then, his arms full of wood, "No. She's just Lilly. She was abandoned when she was a baby, found her sister a few months ago, and then was kidnapped by her parents who brought her on the wagon train. When she got sick, they thought she was going to die, so they let my family have her, and they left the train. We took care of her until she got better. Now she's taking care of me and Clara." After his long tale, Cody appeared to be out of breath, and put the logs down with a sigh, "Well, there are the logs you wanted, Will. What should I do now?"

Will's eyes hadn't left me for the last half of the story. He turned back to Cody, "Uh . . . Yes. Thank you, Cody. Could you get the pot and run to fill it with water?"

"Alright, Will!" Cody grabbed the pot and started upstream to where the water would be cleaner.

I stood bouncing Clara as she cried and Will Haskim started a fire. I hadn't felt the need to tell a stranger the story that had changed my life so drastically. I didn't even want to hear it told! After a moment he asked, "Did Cody's story have any truth to it, Miss Lilly?"

I nodded, "Yes."

He placed a log on the fire, "That's very brave."

When Cody came back, Will put the water over the fire and threw some rice into it for our dinner.

That night, Will insisted Cody and Clara and I sleep in the wagon and he would take the quilt and sleep outside.

It was peaceful, and I finally got to sleep the whole night through. In the morning, I woke to the glorious sound of water flowing over rocks, leaves blowing in the wind, and something else . . . I smelled food. Meat! I wondered how that could be. No one had been behind us in the desert, and the others were far ahead.

Cody and Clara were still asleep. I got dressed quietly and went outside.

The smell of meat was stronger; and as I came around the wagon, I saw it was our own breakfast! Will Haskim stood over a fire. Above it was a metal grate with small strips of meat roasting on it.

I came up beside him. He smiled, "Good morning!"

"Good morning," I said.

He bent down to turn the strips of meat over. The sides he turned up were browned from the fire.

"Where did you get all of this?"

"It's frog from the river." He continued turning the meat, "I figured we all might need the nourishment. It seems you haven't had much to eat for a while. Have you?"

Did he think I hadn't been providing for my family? "What makes you think that?" I asked.

He looked at me over his shoulder, "I think we all look a bit on the bony side."

I didn't know what to say as he took the meat off the grate and put a pot of what appeared to be roots and water on to boil, "For Clara," he explained.

I hadn't meant to be rude, "Is there something I can do to help, Mr. Haskim?"

He straightened, "You can wake up Cody and Clara," he said, "and you can call me Will."

Cody ate his meat quickly, and we all ate some of the roots.

After we ate, Cody went off to play in the river. I was still sitting on the ground near the fire Will was getting ready to put out. He took the last piece of meat off the grate, placed it on a plate with a knife, and sat down beside me, "Do you know how to give this to Clara?"

"I can't," I answered, confused, "She doesn't have any teeth."

He held it out to me, "Scrape the meat until it turns into a paste, then you can give it to her."

He cleaned up and put out the fire while I gave the meat to Clara. I watched him out of the corner of my eye. I wanted to appreciate the relief that was deep inside of me. I felt taken care of, and less afraid of what lie ahead. I wanted to let that security sink in and comfort me, but it didn't yet.

None of us rode in the wagon that day, to spare the oxen while they regained their strength from crossing the desert. They would need it for the miles ahead. Going through the desert had made me forget the mountain we'd have to cross. And winter would be in full swing in the high mountain passes, but I couldn't let myself think of those things yet. We still had nearly seventy miles before reaching the mountains.

But those seventy miles seemed to pass quickly. We made it in a week's time. Will was proving himself useful. He killed frogs to eat nearly every day, took expert care of the oxen, and talked as long as Cody wanted to. I never knew Cody could be so talkative. He seemed to thrive with the constant flow of conversation.

Will and I did little talking, though. I still had a difficult time feeling at ease with him. He seemed aware of my feelings, and gave me time to adjust, which I was thankful for. I found I could act more like myself as each day passed.

All at once, the mountains were before us. The shrubby bushes turned into pine trees as we climbed. The sandy earth turned rocky, and the slopes became more steep.

Snow fell off and on, and we were once again forced to walk beside the wagon, except Cody, who drove.

I continued to carry Clara during the day. She was growing heavier, but she kept warm against me; and I couldn't leave her alone in the back of the wagon.

Within two weeks, we were walking through shallow snow. The wind constantly bit at our chapped faces.

As we were going up a particularly steep slope, one oxen lost his footing and the wagon dropped back several feet. For the rest of that day, Will and I walked on either side of the wagon, guiding it as we made our way up the hill. The trail provided no place to rest that night.

"We'll keep going," I called to Cody. "Maybe there will be a place to rest in the morning."

No such place appeared. The cold of the night froze every part of me. Sometimes I breathed down at Clara's little head to warm her. By morning we could see there would be no stopping for quite some time. My feet dragged in the snow and I bent under Clara's weight.

Finally, we came to a place the oxen would be able to hold the wagon still for a few moments. Cody jumped down. He was beaming, "I drove the team straight through the night, and didn't run into anything!"

I smiled back at him, struggling to open my eyelids after blinking.

Will came around to us after checking the oxen, "We should get moving. They won't be able to hold it long."

Cody and I were silent. We were all tired, but I tried to sound enthusiastic, "Let's go, Cody! He's right. You can keep driving. You're doing a wonderful job!"

I gave him a hug and he smiled before going back to the front. Will stood in front of me, looking down with tired eyes.

"We should keep pushing the wagon," I said.

I tried not to look too exhausted under his scrutinizing gaze. Finally, he spoke, "Let me take Clara."

I started to object but he didn't let me, "You've carried her all this way. You're too worn out."

I wanted to protest but I knew he was right. I couldn't go much longer, and the extra weight was only shortening that time.

I was silent for a moment. Did I trust him with my little baby?

He smiled, "I'll be careful."

I untied the apron and unwrapped it from around me. Clara woke and started to cry. I handed her to Will and watched as he cradled her in his arms and rocked back and forth. Soon, she stopped crying.

He smiled at me, "How do you tie that thing?"

"Hold her against you and I'll tie it."

I wrapped it, and he pulled his hands away and smiled. We looked at each other for a few seconds. He was tall, and almost looked comical with such a small baby strapped against him, but I liked it. I realized I trusted him with her.

The walking was much easier without carrying her. I had done it for so long I'd forgotten what it was like without the extra weight.

We didn't come upon a resting place until late in the evening. I brushed the snow off a fallen pine and dropped onto the log as soon as Cody pulled the wagon to a stop.

Will came around the other side of the wagon. I couldn't help but laugh at him still carrying little Clara against him. My laugh echoed back to us from the trees and mountains. I couldn't remember laughing like that before. Will smiled and came to sit beside me on the log. He looked less tired than he had that morning.

"Do I look that bad?" he asked.

I was still smiling, "No," I shook my head.

"No?" He teased.

Suddenly, shyness overcame me again, "Uh . . . It was just . . . Clara."

He looked down at her and back at my face questioningly.

"She just looks so small with you."

He looked back down at her and touched her head with a large finger, "She is very small." He turned back to me, "You should laugh more often. It's nice." Then he stood up and strode away.

My face felt flushed and for once I was thankful for the cold.

We rested that night and were able to

make much better time as we started the next morning.

The trail started downward and the trees thinned, and we knew we were on the western slopes of the Sierras.

I thought I would feel elation or an overwhelming urge to increase my pace, but I didn't. I didn't believe our journey would ever end. Hills, valleys, deserts, trees, rivers, and endless sky would go on forever.

The nights continued to be cold, but the weather was like spring during the day.

We turned north one evening and set up camp soon after. The night was chilly after a pleasant, sunny day. We lingered around the fire long after supper was finished. The grass was dry, and stars shone clear in the sky. Clara lay half asleep on the old apron on the ground.

Cody moved closer to me, his eyes glowing, "Lilly, it's Christmas Eve."

"Christmas Eve?"

Cody nodded, his eyes still filled with rapture. Will had moved to the other side of me, the same childish joy in his eyes.

Cody spoke in wonder, "You don't know what Christmas is?"

"Yes," I said slowly. "It was right before I was taken away."

Memories faded in and out of my mind. Before the mountains, deserts, and plains; I had lived with my family. I almost felt they had passed on, that they were no more. Could it be that, somewhere behind me, they continued living, working, and loving each other? Loving me. What were they doing while I had been climbing rocky slopes with Cody, Frank, and Harriet? While I crossed miles of plains, and was starving and exhausted in the Forty-Mile Desert?

Tears ran quickly down my cheeks. Cody was searching my face, "What's the matter, Lilly?"

I wiped the tears away, "I'll be alright. I'm just tired."

Will spoke from beside me, "Cody, you run and get ready for bed."

He ran to the wagon after one last look at my eyes. I turned to Will. His face was serious in the firelight, "Are you alright, Lilly?"

"Yes," I answered flatly.

He thought for a moment, "Had you forgotten about your family?"

I stared at him. How could he know? I nodded, and tears started running down my cheeks again, "How could I forget them? They were, they are, my family, but I don't know how to explain it."

"You have another family now?" He looked as though he wanted to cry himself.

"How did you know?" I asked.

He looked into the fire as he spoke, "My parents wanted to go to California. They had heard the weather was like constant spring, and they wanted to start a cattle ranch. My sister and I still lived on their farm and they asked us to come with them. They wanted to live their dream and take us along. We agreed and we wanted to go. We started in the spring. In the middle of the great plains, far from any town, Rocky Mountain spotted fever swept through the camp."

He looked away from the fire and back to me, "My mother didn't suffer long. We buried her in the plains, leaving the miles of wind and sky and grass to surround her for eternity."

He paused.

I wanted to comfort him in some way, but I wasn't sure how. I waited for him to continue.

"When you told me about my father and sister, I thought I couldn't go on without them. Then I saw you, and I decided that if all I could do was help your family, that would be like helping my family. So while you and Cody were washing in the Carson River, I decided to do what I could; but I had no hope for my own future. Then I heard your story, blurted out in all honesty," he added, a corner of his mouth turned up in amusement, "I saw your reaction too. You didn't feel special, or strong, or courageous. I would say that you saw yourself as nearly the opposite."

I almost smiled. I knew he was right. I did see myself as insignificant and weak.

"But that's not what I saw," he continued, "I saw strength and compassion and persistence. I saw a little boy who had so much room for others, and a sweet baby girl," he smiled at Clara, who was asleep then, "And pretty soon, I got busy helping you make it to California, and I didn't think about my family as much. I felt like I had turned my back on them, but I realized I was doing what I was supposed to."

He paused, "Our hearts have to heal, Lilly. We can let them without feeling guilty about it."

I suddenly felt different than I had in a long time, and I didn't feel like crying any more. The thoughts of long ago faded, and the present came alive.

"Thank you, Will," I turned to him and smiled.

We started out early in the morning. We all seemed to have the energy we had lacked for so many days. Each step seemed to mean something; even little Clara squirmed against me.

We walked into a small town late in the afternoon. Will and Cody turned to me with wide smiles spread across their faces.

I looked back and forth between the two, "What is it?"

They both laughed, and Will pointed to a sign we were just passing, "Sutter's Mill!"

I laughed. We were in the town where Cody's aunt and uncle lived!

People on the sidewalks stared at us as we rode down the main street. We were arriving later than any other wagons.

Will pointed out a post office and suggested we go there to ask about Cody's uncle. Cody waited in the wagon with Clara while Will and I stepped inside. A middle-aged man with grey hair stood behind a counter.

"Excuse us, Sir. Could you tell us where we

might find Mr. Thomas Duckson?" Will asked.

"Yes, Sir," he answered. "Head straight out of town and turn left on the first road you come to. Can't miss it."

"Thank you."

The man nodded, "You're welcome. Have a nice day, you two."

Will smiled, "We will. You, as well." He opened the door for me, and we stepped back into the sunlight.

"Where is he?" Cody asked impatiently, handing Clara to me. He had been eager to arrive at his uncle's house all day.

We got up on either side of him, "Just up the street and to the left."

Will drove the wagon. Cody couldn't have done it, with the way he was fidgeting in his seat. We drove several minutes before turning onto a dirt road. A small log cabin sat in the distance with the sun reflecting from its windows.

The wagon rolled into the yard and we came to a stop. Cody climbed over me and ran to the house. He banged on the door until a woman opened it. She stared at him for a moment, then brought him into a hug.

Will and I watched the reunion from the buggy seat. We could hear the woman's voice, "Cody! You're here! You've grown so much in two years."

A man came out and knelt on the ground, bringing Cody against him.

His voice was deep, "We've been waiting

for weeks. We didn't know what to think. All the wagon trains already got here!"

The couple stood, looking toward the wagon, and their smiles faded.

They walked over to us with Cody, "Hello," the man said, "I'm Thomas Duckson." He held his hand up to us. Will reached across me and took it, "Hello, Mr. Duckson. I'm Will Haskim and this is Lilly."

I nodded, "Hello."

"Did you bring Cody?"

Will waited for me to answer. I took a short breath, "Yes, Mr. Duckson. Cody's parents, Frank and Harriet, died of the fever."

I felt like I had struck him. He drew in a quick breath, "I see," he said quietly.

We were silent. Cody stood by his aunt, staring at the ground.

She was the first to speak, "We should get inside. I'm sure you could all use some rest."

"Yes, let's go inside," Cody's uncle agreed.

Cody and I went in with them, while Will took the wagon to the barn to take care of the oxen.

Cody and Clara played for a while, and then both fell asleep in a bundle on the floor. Mr. Duckson carried Cody down the hall into a bedroom and laid him on the large bed. I laid Clara beside him and went back to the front room.

June

I wiped the tears from my eyes. I had finally been able to get a breath from laughing, "That can't be true!"

Elias Smothers leaned casually against the back of the couch, "Who knows," he shrugged, "I guess you'll have to decide for yourself."

"Oh, come on!" Margret laughed out loud, "What happened after the raccoon jumped on your head?"

Elias turned his dark blue eyes to her and suddenly burst out laughing, "That, Miss Margret, shall remain a mystery."

We all laughed again.

Throughout the evening, I had started to wonder if I had been wrong about Margret. She seemed at least slightly taken with Elias Smothers.

I didn't wonder why though. Jacob had told me he was handsome, and I was sure Margret would have to agree.

He had a strong jaw and an openness behind his eyes that made him seem as trustworthy as a child.

I think we were all disappointed when he stood to leave.

Margret and Jacob followed him to the door,

while Joshua and Meg came into the kitchen to help me with the dishes. I stood there listening with little Miriam in my arms as the others started cleaning up.

"Thank you for coming tonight," I heard Jacob say.

"Thank you for having me. You have a lovely family."

I peeked around the door frame so I could see them.

Elias turned to Margret. He smiled a little hesitantly, "I would be very happy if you would go on a picnic with me Sunday, Margret."

I wished I could see Margret's face, but her back was turned to me.

"I would like that," Margret said. "Thank you for asking."

I could hear her smile as she talked. Elias smiled back, "Good! I'll come for you around noon."

He smiled one more time at Jacob, "I'll see you in town."

The door shut and Margret turned around and saw me looking in. She grinned, walked lightly past me into the kitchen, and plunged her hands into the dish water.

Lilly

Will was just coming in when I got back from putting Cody and Clara to bed.

I smiled at him, "They're asleep."

He smiled back, "Good, they needed it."

We both sat down across from the Ducksons. Will put his arm behind me, along the back of the couch. I looked at Thomas Duckson. He could have been Frank's twin, only he was a little older.

His wife, Alice, was somewhat thin, had light brown hair and green eyes.

She leaned forward, "Thank you so much for taking care of Cody. We can see how well he's done with you."

I smiled, "I've loved being with him."

Thomas put his arm around his wife and she leaned against him, "Well, he seems to get along with your little one."

"They've been just like brother and sister," Will answered.

"I'm glad," Alice said, "I'm sure it was good for him . . . after losing his parents."

We were silent for a moment. Thomas seemed to be taking his brother's death well, but there was pain behind his watery blue eyes. He seemed to feel the hurt more deeply for a time, but spoke after a long, deep sigh, "So, how long have you two been married?"

I stared at him in disbelief. What could have given him the idea we were married?

Will and I turned to each other. He hastily pulled his arm out from behind me and put his hands together in his lap, "Uh, Sir, Lilly and I . . . I mean, we . . ." His weather worn face grew red. I felt the same shade creeping up my own neck.

I took over, "I found him in the desert. His family was gone and no one else stopped to help."

The Ducksons looked startled, "We just assumed . . . you seem so . . ." Alice started, "But what about Clara?"

"Cody and I took her in when her parents were killed by wolves. That was long before we found Will."

"Oh, I see," she said thoughtfully, easing back into her seat.

We sat in silence for a time before Thomas spoke, "We all better get some rest. It's been a long evening. Lilly, you can sleep with the children. We have a lean-to with a cot you can stay in, Will."

Will nodded, "Thank you." He stood, walked to the door, and turned, "Goodnight Thomas, Miss Alice." He paused and nodded to me, "Lilly."

"Goodnight, Will."

He went out and shut the door behind him.

The confusion I felt from our previous

conversation hung heavily in my mind. I didn't know what to say, so I took Will's example, "I better get to bed myself!" I stood, and they stood with me.

"Yes," Alice smiled, "We all should." She gave me a hug, "Goodnight, Dear."

I left them and quietly walked into the room where Cody and Clara were sleeping. I lay down beside Clara, her little body resting peacefully. I wondered what we would do in that place. What life would give us there.

I thought of Will. Thomas and Alice thought we were married, thought we loved each other! I couldn't imagine what it would be like to love a person like a wife should. Yet, Will . . . I relied on him; I trusted him.

I woke up and stretched. No one was beside me. Where were Cody and Clara? Cody never woke before me, and he'd certainly never leave the wagon. I opened my eyes. I was in a room. There was a small window where sunlight poured onto the quilt spread across the bed.

Everything came back from the night before. I hurried to dress and go out into the kitchen.

Alice stood at the stove. She turned as I walked in, and a smile lit her face, "Good morning, Lilly!"

"Good morning, Alice." I sat at the table and she set a plate of flapjacks in front of me, "You must have slept well. It's going on eight o'clock."

I took a bite of the warm food she'd given

me, "Where are Cody and Clara?" I asked.

"They had breakfast and went out to see Will. They're chopping wood. They're around back if you want to help after you've eaten."

I finished breakfast and went out back. The air was crisp, the sky blue; and the sound of an ax splitting wood rang through the yard.

As I came around the side of the house, Cody came across the yard to me and put Clara into my outstretched arms, "Hi, baby!" I laughed and twirled around with her.

Cody laughed too, "Lilly, Uncle Tom is teaching us how to cut wood. Will's taking the first turn, and he's going to teach me what I can do to help!"

"That's wonderful, Cody!" I stood with Clara on my hip and walked closer to Will. He placed a log on a tree stump and swung the ax expertly above his head and down through the wood.

I spoke above the ring of the ax, "I hear you're learning how to chop wood."

He smiled as I came nearer, "I'm sure Cody will learn faster than I am." He swung, and another two perfectly even pieces of wood lay at his feet.

Thomas came up to Cody, who was standing beside me, "Are you ready to learn some wood splitting?"

I turned to him, "Are you sure Cody is ready for an ax, Thomas?"

"Wood splitting isn't all done with an ax.

We're going to use a wedge and hammer. And, please, call me Tom."

I sighed, "I see, Tom. I think Cody would do very well with that."

Tom took Cody to a fallen tree further out in the yard. I watched as he showed Cody how to use a two-man saw. When they had sawed part of the way through, Tom stuck an iron wedge into it, Cody struck it with a heavy mallet, and the two sides fell apart.

He called to me, "Lilly, did you see? Did you see me split the wood?"

"Yes, it was wonderful!" I laughed.

Will smiled at me and wiped the sweat from his forehead, "You seem energetic today."

I bounced Clara on my hip, "I guess I am." I bit my lip and smiled. I felt happy, and at home.

For the next few days we settled into our new home and worked alongside Tom and Alice. They were two of the kindest people I had ever met. They were so much like Frank and Harriet that sometimes I wondered if it would remind Cody too much of his parents.

But he seemed to thrive with them. He loved his aunt and uncle, and I could see they cared for him; but they let me continue to act as his guardian. They seemed to understand the bond that made us a family. I came to realize more fully that I would be responsible for raising Cody and Clara.

Sometimes I wondered if we should have a home of our own, but I saw bonds forming once again that created a family. The healing Will spoke of that night on the trail manifested itself full force in that home.

Tom loved Cody deeply and would often ask for his help with chores or teach him a new skill. I also enjoyed time with Tom, and felt as though he could be my own uncle.

Alice was a natural-born homemaker and an amazing cook. She kept all our clothes mended and the house scrubbed clean. She told me over and over how lovely it was to have a woman to talk to. Apparently, women were decidedly scarce in the valley.

Will worked hard, helped Tom with his tasks, and had more respect for Alice than most people did for anybody. He grew closer to Cody and Clara every day. Cody stuck to his side, and he loved every minute of it.

Cody was impressed with everything Will did, and Clara clung to him just as much as she did to me. He would lift her above his head and make faces at her. It made me laugh every time, and then he'd look down at me with his deep brown eyes.

Two weeks after our arrival, I sat at a window in the front room, watching the rain running down the glass. It had been raining for days. Almost all outdoor work had ceased, and there was only so much this many people could do in one small house.

Everyone was seated around the room. I turned away from the window, "Does it always rain so much in California?"

Alice looked up from her book, "Oh, no, Dear. It's rained some in January before, but nothing like this." She noticed my downcast face, "Don't worry. I'm sure the sun will show itself soon." She turned back to her book.

Will glanced up as I was studying the binding of the book he held, "Why don't you read something, Lilly? There are some good books over there."

I glanced at the shelf, wishing I didn't have to tell him I couldn't do what everyone else could.

I spoke slowly, "I don't know."

He got out of his seat, grabbed a red-covered book off the shelf and thrust it into my hands, "Read this. It's one of my favorites."

I didn't open the thick book in my hands, and his smile faded, "What's the matter? Don't you like that one?"

"It's not that. It's just that I can't read this." I offered the book back to him, "I never learned how." I looked at it, remembering how June promised to teach me to read.

He took it, his face blank.

Everyone in the room looked at me. Cody spoke first, "You don't know how to read? How come?"

"My Aunt said I had no need of other people's ideas. My sister was going to start teaching me last Christmas," I answered.

Will looked eagerly down at me, "I'll teach you."

"You will?"

He laughed, "Of course!"

We started that night. While everyone was in the kitchen fixing dinner, Will and I sat on the couch.

"Do you know your letters?" he asked.

"I know what letters are," I said hopefully.

"Good! We'll start with learning each letter. There are twenty-six of them." He took a sheet of paper and a pen, and wrote something on it, "This is called 'A'."

I learned one letter and then another, until supper was ready. The rain continued, and each evening was free for Will to teach me. I learned each letter, and then we began putting them together into words.

After my lessons, Will would get out the book he had said was his favorite. I sat by him, leaning over the book and he ran his finger beneath the words as he read them.

The book was a made-up story. Will explained to me how a man had imagined the characters and events and had written them in a way meant to help us see it all in our own imaginations. Ideas were expressed by what the people in the story did and said.

One evening Tom came back from the post office and stepped inside, "The rain stopped. I heard that Sacramento has flooded. Whole sections of the city are washed out!"

Alice frowned, "We can be thankful it didn't make it all the way out here. All those people must be suffering terribly."

"Yes, and now that it's stopped raining, we can start planting."

"What do you grow?" Will asked.

"Summer squash to sell, and other vegetables for ourselves."

A thrill of excitement ran through me, "I love planting!"

Will's eyes sparkled, "Me too."

June

Margret and Elias were walking up the road, talking amiably. I was sitting on the front porch.

As they got closer, I could hear Margret's hearty laugh and the murmur of Elias's deep voice.

I stood and watched them come. Elias tipped his hat as they stopped in front of me.

"How was your walk?" I asked.

"It was very nice." Margret smiled up at him.

"It was," he agreed, "but I have to go now. I have to get to work. Good evening, Ladies," he nodded, smiled at Margret, and turned to the road.

We both watched him go for a moment, then I turned to Margret, "A picnic and four walks in the last two weeks?" I teased, "Are you two courting, or preparing your legs for a journey?"

Margret glanced thoughtfully in the direction Elias had gone, "I'm not sure," she bit her lip, then smiled, "He's awfully kind. We walked through town today. There was a woman carrying her baby and some packages. When he saw her, he took my hand and we ran across the street to help. We carried her things all the way home for her. It was nice." She sighed, "I'm happy when I'm with him."

"I see that."

"I've never courted before." She giggled, "I've hardly even thought about it." Her smooth forehead crumpled a little, "I'm afraid I won't know how to go about it."

"Oh, Margret," I couldn't help but laugh as I pulled her into a hug, "You're a wonderful person! All that matters is that you care about each other!" I pulled away from her to look at her face, "It sounds like you have a good start down that road already."

"We do." She laughed her full, rippling laugh, "I'm going to see what Meg is doing. I promised to help her with arithmetic when I got back."

Lilly

The days were hot, and the grass was dry. Tom, Will, and Cody worked endlessly at plowing the fifteen acres of ground we needed. I walked from the house into the field with Clara, carrying water to them. We still had time in the evening to relax and have dinner together, and Will continued my reading lessons.

Alice came into my room one morning and touched my arm. She was still in her night gown, "Wake up, Lilly. Will is waiting in the kitchen. He asked me to come get you."

I slipped out from between Cody and Clara, dressed quickly, and went out to the kitchen. Will stood over the table in the faint early morning light.

"What are you doing?" I whispered, "Alice said you wanted me."

He smiled widely, "We're going to plant squash."

I looked at the table. There were two plates of pancakes and eggs.

He pulled a chair out for me, "I made breakfast."

We sat down across from each other. The food was delicious. The pancakes were light, and the omelet was flavorful.

"For some reason, I thought you could only make soup and grilled frog."

He smiled back at me, "I didn't have a kitchen on the trail."

After breakfast, we went into the field. Tom had already tied several sacks of seeds to his horse, "Good morning! Will, you and Lilly can go out on this horse and get started. I'll load up another and be right behind you."

I stepped over to the horse and grabbed its reins, getting ready to pull myself onto its back, but Will walked up behind me. He put his hands on my waist and I looked over my shoulder, "You don't think I can get up on a horse myself," I teased.

His head tilted back and he laughed, "No, I'm positive you can, Lilly." He easily lifted me off the ground and onto the horse's back. He looked up at me from the ground, "I was only trying to be a gentleman." Then he swung himself onto the horse and reached past me for the reins, "I occasionally am one, you know," he said softy.

I glanced back, "You always are," I smiled.

He grinned and flicked the reigns.

I turned to look forward. My cheeks suddenly felt very warm.

Will and I rode to the far end of the field and got down from the horse. He handed me a spade with a long handle, "You can dig, I'll drop the seeds in."

I pushed the shovel into the tilled earth at

the end of the first row, held the dirt back while Will dropped two seeds in, and pulled the shovel out. We went a couple of feet down the row to plant the next seeds.

It felt good to put my shovel into the earth. Everything was good; the sun on my back as it rose, the acres of dirt, and helping Will.

Tom worked at the other end of the field and planned to meet us in the middle. Hours later, Will glanced at the sun, "Looks like lunch time," he looked to Tom who had just stopped to eat.

"Did you bring lunch for us?" I asked.

"Yes," he smiled. He got the saddlebag and pulled out jerky, biscuits, and two canteens.

Will picked up the shovel when we had finished, "I can take a turn digging and you can do the seeds if you want."

I looked at the heavy bag of seeds, then at the blisters forming on my hands, "Alright," I agreed.

We went through two bags of seeds before going home for supper that night.

I couldn't keep my eyes open for my reading lesson. I must have fallen asleep on Will's shoulder.

Someone was picking me up. It was Will. He held me easily, and carried me down the hall. He set me down beside Cody and Clara in the bed and shut the door quietly as he left.

We finished planting the next day. When we met Tom in the center row of the field, we stood looking at our work in the waning light.

Tom put an arm around each of us, "You two make a great team. That's some mighty fine planting!"

Will looked past Tom to me, "In a few months, we'll have hundreds of fresh summer squash, Lilly. Planted with our own hands." He raised his eyebrows, and I giggled.

We stood quietly for another moment. Finally, I asked something I'd been wondering the whole time we were planting, "Will," I paused, "what's a squash?"

Both men turned to me and started laughing.

One evening, about a month after planting, Will and I were having our reading lesson, everyone else was reading their own books, and Clara played on the floor at our feet.

Suddenly, Will looked up, "Let's go for a walk." He shut the book without waiting for me to answer, took my hand, and pulled me to my feet.

I called back to Cody on our way out the door, "Watch your sister."

Will shut the door behind us. He kept my hand in his as we went out onto the main street. Occasionally someone else walked past us, but the night was quiet and there was a faint smell of smoke in the air.

"What are we doing, Will?"

"I just wanted to take a walk with you."

"Alright." I decided to let him work out whatever was on his mind before trying to talk. We were coming to the center of town, with lighted windows and laughing children.

"Have you ever thought of having your own family, Lilly?" Will asked suddenly.

The question took me by surprise, "I have a family. You, Tom and Alice, and the kids."

"But what about a home and family of your own?" he persisted. Then he paused, "Have you ever thought of courting?"

"Not much I guess," I answered without thinking. We stopped and I looked at him, "Have you?"

He held my gaze, "Not until lately."

We stood silently. I didn't know how to respond and he didn't seem to feel the need to go on.

The quiet was broken by a rider racing through town, whipping his horse and calling out, "Fire in Sacramento!"

People came running out onto the street. The man stopped his horse and continued shouting the news, "There's been a fire in Sacramento! Whole streets burned to the ground."

Just as suddenly as the street filled, the people dispersed after hearing the news. Will took my hand and guided me to where the man had just tied up his horse. He took his hat off as we came up to him.

"Hello," Will offered him his hand, "I'm Will Haskim."

The man took it and nodded, "Crew Gentry."

"Is the fire out?" Will asked.

The man scratched his head, "I suppose so. It took me over a day to get here. It's over forty miles, you know. The fire looked as if it was just beginning to dwindle when I left."

"We're sorry about all the damage it caused."

"Well, that's nice of you. Most folks won't be. There'll be an awful lot of work to be done in the city in the coming months. People are willing to pay to get it done too. Most will be more than happy that something happened to give them work."

Will frowned, "I see. Well, I wish you luck on your ride, Mr. Gentry."

"Thank you, Mr. Haskim. I wish you and your wife a good night."

Will was preoccupied and didn't bother correcting the man. He kept my hand in his all the way home, and when we got to the door he just said, "Good night, Lilly. Thank you for the walk," and was gone.

The next morning, Tom and Cody had gone out to work; and Clara was running all through the house. I had started working in the kitchen when Alice came in with solemn eyes. She reached into her apron pocket, pulled out a note, and handed it to me silently.

On the outside was my name in Will's handwriting. I opened it quickly. He wouldn't use any words I didn't know, so I'd be able to read it myself.

Lilly,

I left this morning to ride to Sacramento with Mr. Gentry. I'm going to work there for a while. It's been a long time since I had a job. I hope you understand.

I also hope you know how much I care for Cody and Clara, and for you.

I'll miss you every day, Lilly.

Will

Alice had been watching my face as I read, "Will gave it to Tom before leaving this morning. How long will he be gone?"

I refolded the letter, "I don't know. He's going to work in Sacramento, rebuilding after the fire there."

I went outside and walked through the field of young squash Will and I had planted together.

I felt lonely, but not upset. I understood he needed to work and earn a living. I had known the day would come when he would have to move on. He wasn't the kind of man to stay under someone else's roof the rest of his life.

Cody was just sitting down to breakfast when I got back to the house, and Clara was playing on the floor. I sat down and lifted her into my lap.

Cody was enthusiastic for the day, as usual, "I want to help Will with the watering today!" he said

I looked at him, "Cody," I stopped. I knew

he would be upset to hear that Will was gone, "Cody, your Uncle Tom and I will be watering today."

"Why? What's Will doing?"

"He . . . he's gotten a job in Sacramento."

He looked worried, "Will he come back?"

"Of course, Cody. He'll just be gone for a little while, until things are rebuilt after the fire."

He pushed the food around on his plate, "Oh."

The house was quiet for several weeks. There was more work to be done with Will gone. Cody helped Tom more than ever, and I saw that he was quickly growing up. I helped water the squash every morning and spent the rest of the day with Alice. Clara needed nearly constant attention as she ran from room to room and all around the yard. Her favorite toys were rocks and sticks and dirt.

My evenings felt empty without the reading lessons. I sat and read a book silently with everyone else, but it was lonely without Will reading over my shoulder or his finger traveling across the page.

The plants continued to grow, and for weeks we worked dozens of summer squash into our meals; soup, roasted, or dried squash, or just eaten raw.

The entire family spent most of the time searching for the biggest ones to pick. At the end of the day we'd take out the ones we wanted for ourselves and Tom would drive the rest into town to sell.

The last load of the year was picked at the end of September. When it was packed in crates and loaded into the wagon bed, Tom smiled, "That's the last load. This one goes all the way to Sacramento. We picked them early so they'd make the trip."

My smile froze, "You're taking them to Sacramento?"

"Yes," he paused, "I could look for Will while I'm there, but Sacramento is a big city, Lilly."

Hope welled up inside me, "He'll be where they're rebuilding."

"I'll ask around, but I can't promise anything."

Was it silly to hope he would find him in such a large city? I couldn't help smiling "I know. Thank you."

Instead of reading that night I wrote a letter.

Will,

If you're reading this, you've seen Tom. I hope he found you happy and healthy, and I hope you've been enjoying your work.

I miss our reading lessons and helping you in the fields.

We've had squash in almost all our suppers, and Tom has sold many loads of them. Now I know exactly what a squash is!

Cody wishes you were here. He's grown a lot

these past few months. Clara misses you too.

I hope you can come back soon. I understand you need to work, but I miss you every day. I care about you, and would like to continue the conversation we began the night before you left.

Lilly

I gave it to Tom before going to bed, "Could you give this to Will if you find him?"

He took it, his eyes watching my own, "I'll do my best, Lilly"

I smiled, "I know you will."

Tom returned two weeks later. He arrived late at night. I woke up early the next morning and hurried into the kitchen. He and Alice were sitting at the table.

"Did you see Will?" I asked quickly.

"Yes," Tom stood and dug in his pocket, "He gave me this," he held out a letter.

"Thank you, Tom!" I ran back to my room, and opened the dirt-smudged envelope.

Lilly,

I nearly fell over when I saw Tom coming down the street. I asked him first thing how you and the kids were getting on, and I was overjoyed for your letter. I miss the reading lessons too and hope to get back to them soon.

The city is nearly rebuilt. I'm coming back as soon as my work on this last building is done.

I'm looking forward to finishing our

conversation too.
    Start looking for me in two weeks!
    Will

I watched for him from that moment on. I looked out the window as I kneaded bread dough, or mopped the floor, and looked up from my reading in the evening to search the darkened road.

June

The weeks passed quickly. Summer cooled into autumn, and autumn into winter. Miriam grew quickly and was the happiest baby girl. Elias spent more and more time with our family as he and Margret became closer.

"Did you leave Miriam with Meg?" Jacob asked as I walked into the jailhouse one morning.

"Yes, I dropped them both off to spend the day with Mrs. Bradley at the orphanage. They're having a field trip to study animal tracks outside of town. Apparently, it can't be missed!"

Jacob laughed, "They should enjoy that!"

I crossed the room to stand behind him, "What are you doing spending the morning behind your desk?" I asked as I began to rub his shoulders.

He leaned back in his chair and let his eyelids close for a moment, "The county sent me a bunch of mail this morning."

He leaned forward, and shuffled the stacks of paper around on his desk, "News about who's been arrested, new defensive techniques for lawmen, a dozen wanted posters."

He smiled back at me, "Obviously, they believe your husband has a lot to catch up on."

I went around to stand in front of his desk,

and put my hands on my hips, "Maybe you do at that."

"Not you too!"

"No, no," I waved my finger back and forth, "I've dealt with many schoolboys, and I know how to handle them."

He stood from his chair, and straightened to his full height, "Do you now?"

"Yes," a small laugh escaped, "I do."

"Indeed." He sauntered around the desk to stand in front of me, "I think you don't." He scooped me up quickly in both arms, and spun around.

"I know how to handle school teachers too," he said when he stopped spinning.

I laughed, "Get back to your desk, Sheriff Plyer."

He set me back down on my own two feet and returned to his chair, with a smirk still playing across his lips.

As he started sorting through the papers again, his mouth stiffened, and he quickly looked up at me.

"Jacob, what is it?"

He slowly turned the paper he was holding so I could see it.

Across the top, in large red lettering, was printed, "WANTED".

Beneath the word was a man's face. Dark blue eyes seemed to glare at me above a thick beard. I was terrified to realize, that beard looked to be covering a strong, square jawline.

Elias Smothers was wanted!

"I don't believe it." I looked from the poster back to Jacob's face, "Jacob!"

He got up and stormed around the desk, "It is. He's a con man and a kidnapper!" He slammed his fist down on the paper and looked up suddenly, "Where's Margret?"

"Oh, no! Jacob, she was going to meet Elias at the brook and go on to the Widow Shore's place to do some chores for her."

"How long ago was that?" Jacob hurried to put on his hat and coat.

"About half an hour. They should be at Widow Shore's by now."

"I'm going there. You go to the brook!" He stormed out before I could answer. I ran out the door and down the road toward the brook.

I stepped into the trees and slowed down when I got close enough to hear voices.

I finally got to where I could see through the trees. Margret and Elias were standing beside each other at the edge of the brook.

Elias was smiling at her, "I'm not sure I believe you."

Her back straightened slightly, "Oh, don't you?"

"Fine," he took a step closer to the frozen brook. "But I think we'll fall."

Margret laughed, and stepped daringly onto the ice.

Elias seemed to take a breath before stepping out next to her. I stared at the back of his head. I shivered and pulled my coat more tightly around me.

I needed to get Jacob, but I couldn't leave Margret alone with that man. I turned to look back through the trees toward the road and was startled to see Jacob standing behind me.

"Jacob!" I gasped.

He covered my mouth quickly with his hand, "I just got here," he whispered. His lips were a tight line. He lowered his hand and nodded toward the couple, "What are they doing on the ice?"

I stared up at him, "Sliding."

Just when we turned back to the brook, Elias tried to slide forward, and fell hard on the ice. He cringed, but Margret threw her head back and laughed, "You're right. You shouldn't be on the ice!"

Margret offered him her small hand. He took it, but I noticed he didn't put any weight on it as he lifted himself up. He looked down at Margret with a big smile, and they laughed together.

"We should get going to Mrs. Shore's place," Elias said. They stepped back onto the bank.

Jacob touched my arm, "I'm going in," he mouthed.

I turned toward the couple.

Elias took her hand in his. He was looking tenderly down into her grey eyes, "Margret."

Jacob stepped past me.

Elias was still talking, "I think ---"

Jacob was on top of him, standing between him and Margret. Jacob pulled Elias's arms behind him, and forced him to the ground.

I ran out to Margret.

She looked frantic, "What's going on." She pulled away from me, "Jacob! What are you doing?"

"He's wanted, Margret. He's a criminal."

"I can explain!" Elias moaned as Jacob clamped a pair of handcuffs tightly around his wrists, "You have to hear the whole story."

Jacob leaned closer to his ear, "Save it for when we get to town," he said quietly.

Margret and I walked back through town, trailing a little way behind the two men. Jacob didn't usually get angry with offenders, but he had been afraid for Margret. I hoped she could see that.

Jacob sat Elias down on a three-legged stool in the center of the jailhouse, his arms still fastened behind him.

Jacob stood directly in front of him, "Why don't you start by telling us about the kidnapping?"

Margret and I stood behind Jacob's desk. Elias glanced at us and back to Jacob, "I'm not a criminal. I was working undercover when those charges were filed against me." He sighed, "I was a sheriff in St. Louis."

"St. Louis? That's a big town, Elias. They would get someone older and more experienced to be sheriff."

Elias shrugged.

It was Jacob's turn to sigh, "Well, if you were a sheriff, you know I can't go by what you tell me. I'll have to lock you up until I can check with St. Louis."

Elias nodded, "I know."

Jacob sent a letter and we waited.

I took food to the jail for Elias every day. Margret never went with me.

We couldn't be certain he was a criminal. But, if he had been a sheriff doing undercover work, why was he wanted?

They would have known about the work he was doing and not pressed charges.

My shoulders dropped as I made breakfast. He was guilty. That's all there was to it. I raised the spoon I was using to stir the pancake batter and slammed it back down. It wasn't right! I didn't understand how people could be so cruel.

He was a kidnapper! How could anyone do that? I paused. An image of my father's angry face came to mind.

Lilly

Two weeks passed, then three, then four. Will didn't come. Alice and Tom tried to comfort me. They said construction was unpredictable and he would probably ride up the road any day, but he didn't.

One night, after two months of waiting, Tom came home from the store in town. He looked disturbed and barely said a word all evening.

I put Cody and Clara to bed quietly and went back out to sit by the fire with Tom and Alice. Tom finally spoke, "Lilly, I have some news."

Alice had been quiet that evening as well, "What is it?" I asked.

"In town today, they were saying there's been an epidemic of Cholera in Sacramento. It was brought by a ship."

My heart beat faster then seemed to stop. Was that why Will hadn't come? It seemed to be the only reasonable explanation.

I waited for another week, but I had to find out. I decided that if something had happened to Will, I wanted to return to Jacob and June.

I told Tom and Alice that I would be going to Sacramento, "I don't want to leave you, but I have to find out."

"We understand, Lilly," Tom's deep voice was sympathetic.

I hated to tell them the next part, "And if he's not there, I want to go back to my family. There are ships that come to Sacramento from New York. I can take one back."

"Will you be wanting to take the children with you?" Alice asked quietly.

I would have loved to take them with me, but I couldn't make that decision. Cody was their nephew, and I couldn't bear the thought of separating him and Clara. But I felt they were my own children and wouldn't be able to leave them.

"I can't make that decision. Cody is your nephew."

They looked at each other. Neither spoke, but it seemed they knew the other's thoughts. "Lilly, he's yours now. He became yours long before you arrived here," Alice's voice was calm, "We love you all, but whatever you do, you need to do it together. Talk to Cody, he's old enough to know what he wants."

A tear rolled down my cheek. They loved him enough to let him go. Would they ever know what that meant to me? Nothing I could say would be sufficient, "Thank you. I'll talk to him in the morning."

Cody was watering the horses the next morning. I went out to meet him as he came back to the house, "Cody, walk in the fields with me?"

His eyebrows drew together, "Alright."

The squash vines had long since been tilled under, and dust blew as we stepped through the dirt. I was afraid to start, afraid of what his answer might be. "Cody, I need to find Will. I have to know if something has happened to him." I stopped and turned to him, "I need to go to Sacramento."

"You should, and I want to go with you," he broke in.

"I want you to, but if I don't find Will . . . I'll be returning to my family. The family I was taken from."

Cody's eyes were grave, he seemed to be searching within himself, and within me, "You don't want to take us with you?"

"I want to, Cody. I want you and Clara with me more than anything, but you have a home here, and your aunt and uncle. And I'll be going on a ship all the way to New York."

I looked at him. His face was nearly level with my own. It showed maturity, his hands were stronger and his shoulders broader now. He'd grown during the past year, "You have to decide, Cody. I want to be a family, but I also know you have a family here."

"You and Clara and Will are my family. I love my aunt and uncle, but I have to stay with our family."

I blinked back tears and hugged him, "I'm so glad."

We spent the rest of the morning helping Tom and Alice with the chores, and the afternoon and evening packing and preparing for our journey. We had very little; a couple changes of clothing, a few dishes, an iron pot, a metal rack for cooking over a fire, enough food for the two days' ride to Sacramento, and our canteens full of water. Will had all of his things with him.

We woke early the next morning. The sun shone through the crisp December air, and the wind blew as we loaded the two horses Tom and Alice had given us. I wrapped Harriet's old apron around Clara and me when everything was loaded. At a year and eight months she was much heavier.

Hugging his aunt and uncle, Cody seemed to realize he would probably never see them again. He clung to Alice for a long time before turning to his uncle. Tom looked like he wanted to hold his nephew forever, "You're quite the young man, Cody. Take good care of your family, and know your Uncle Tom and you are doing the same thing." He smiled, "Maybe we'll come see you someday."

Cody nodded, holding back tears, "I will, Uncle Tom."

Cody got up on his horse. I hugged Tom, then Alice. Her eyes were moist. She wasn't only crying for her nephew, but for me, "I've loved having you here, Lilly."

Tom put his arm around her, "We both have."

I wrapped my arms around them both and held on for a moment. What was I doing leaving a home and family who loved me and my children? I had to build a home and family of my own, and the first step toward that was finding what had become of Will.

I held them away from me, "Thank you both."

It took two days to ride to Sacramento. It felt natural being on the trail again.

Sacramento lay in a valley. From the nearby hill, we could see streets lined with homes and many larger buildings.

We spent three weeks walking around Sacramento, searching the face of every man we passed, and asking anyone who would listen if they had seen a man by Will's description.

I also inquired when the ships in the harbor would set sail for New York. All of them gave the same answer; "After the Christmas holiday."

I didn't want to leave while there was any hope of finding Will, but was there really hope anymore?

The Cholera had swept through the city like a fog. No home had gone untouched, many doctors had died of the disease, hospitals had been filled to capacity, and the cemeteries had many freshly laid mounds of dirt and shining, new headstones. The sight of the graves made me cringe.

Cody and Clara and I slept near the wharf each night, and left early each morning so no one would notice us.

Christmas day came quickly. I would have to speak to someone about passage on a ship, but I didn't know who. After searching one street that morning, we came back past the wharf on our way to a nearby hospital to check their records.

As we passed, I saw the back of a tall man with broad shoulders and dark hair looking at a shipping crate. My heart leaped into my throat, and I took off through the crowd, shouting, "Will! Will!"

I left Cody and Clara far behind and flew into Will's arms as he turned around.

I buried my face against him, sobbing as he put his arms around me, "Oh, Will, I thought I'd never see you again. I thought the Cholera had taken you!"

He bent down and kissed my cheek.

Suddenly I realized how I'd thrown myself at him in the middle of a crowded wharf, and he'd kissed me in front of everyone!

I pulled away, "Will, what are you . . ." the words died on my lips as I looked up.

It wasn't Will! The young man smiled down at me mockingly.

I tried to speak, but the words wouldn't come. The stranger's arms were still around me. I quickly pulled out of them, and we stood staring at each other.

At that moment, Cody and Clara broke through the crowd.

Cody was smiling until he realized it was a stranger and not Will, "Oh," he said flatly, "Who's this?"

When I didn't answer, the man did, "I'm a friend of your sister's."

Cody stared at me, and the young man smiled widely. I took my horse's reins from Cody's hand, "We should go." I nodded to the man as we turned to go, "Good day, friend."

We hurried to the hospital. I couldn't stop thinking of the man until we approached the nurse at the front desk. She smiled brightly, "What can I do for you today, miss?"

"I'm looking for someone who might have been sick."

"Alright," the woman answered in a light voice, "Do you know when they were here?"

"No," feelings of despair rushed through me as I thought again of how little I knew, or would probably ever know, "I'm not sure he was even here. I wonder if you could check your records?"

"I can do that. What's the man's name?"

"Will Haskim," I answered.

The woman spent a long time searching through files, drawers and cabinets. Finally, she read to me from a paper, "Here we are. Will Haskim; 27 years old, six feet, two inches tall, brown hair, brown eyes. Is this the one, Miss?"

I swallowed with difficulty and felt my heart in my throat, "That's him. What does it say?"

"It says, 'Will Haskim volunteered here, helping to care for several dozen Cholera patients before contracting the disease himself on the 18th of December, 1850. He wasn't admitted and hasn't returned." She looked up, "That's all we have on a Will Haskim, Miss." She saw my downcast face, "I'm sorry," she finished quietly.

I couldn't feel anything, yet I felt everything. Will was gone forever. I didn't want to imagine the rest of my life without him.

Somehow, we got back to the wharf. Cody sat down beside me, and I took Clara out of her wrap and let her play on the ground. Cody watched her. He was hurting too.

We stayed on the wharf until evening, when I finally woke out of my mourning. I tied Clara back onto me and stood, "We're going to sail on the first ship out, Cody. Come with me."

We went to the small white-washed building on the wharf. Several sailors were inside, and an important looking man was talking to them. I left Cody and Clara outside with the horses. When I walked in, the room went silent.

My cheeks reddened as I faced the group. I decided to address the important looking man wearing a suit, "I would like passage on the next ship to New York."

The man waited a moment to answer, "On your own?"

"No, Sir. Two children will be with me."

"You want to sail to New York?"

"Yes, Sir," I answered with more confidence than I felt, "I do."

The men burst into laughter. "Listen, sweetheart, nobody sails to New York except sailors," a rough looking man scoffed. "No women will be aboard any of those ships,"

I kept my attention on the one in the suit, "How much will it cost?"

"Usually around $300, going through Panama."

I felt my face freeze, "$300?"

"That's right," the men laughed again.

Suddenly a deep voice spoke behind me, "Go easy on her, boys."

The man in the suit answered, "It's not me. It's just the way it is."

The young man stepped past me and stuffed a handful of money into the other man's suit pocket. It was the one I'd hugged on the wharf, "Now she rides," he said.

The group of men stared at us as the man led me out of the building.

Once we were outside I turned to him, "Why did you do that?"

He shrugged, "I had the money. You'll be going the long way though, around Cape Horn in South America. Board that ship in the morning," he pointed to a large ship at anchor in the harbor. The prow read, 'The Noble'. "And don't be late," he warned, "it won't wait for you."

He smiled and sauntered away. I went back to Cody and Clara, wondering if I felt comfortable with his paying our passage, and why he would do such a thing.

"We've got a ship to sail on," I said to Cody as soon as I reached him. He smiled. It would be a relief to get out of that city and on our way.

It was cold that night, and the wind blew wildly along the wharf. I tossed and turned for hours, but sometime during the night, I was able to fall into a deeper sleep hugging Clara close to my body.

When I woke up, I found a thick blanket draped over the three of us. It was old and grey and had the initials M. B. on one corner.

Sailors were already working on deck when we came up the ship's gangplank, leading our horses. Clara was tied to me as usual, and Cody walked beside me. When we reached the top, a large, rough looking sailor stepped in front of us. He was middle-aged and spoke in a raspy voice, "No passengers going on this trip, Missy."

"But I---"

"No. Just turn yourself around and go on home."

Just then, the man that paid our passage came up behind us. He spoke loudly, "Let them on board, Sailor. Their fare has been paid."

The sailor quickly obeyed and went away, mumbling under his breath.

The man led us aboard and directed us to the rail of the ship, "You can stay here until we get underway. Now, what about these horses?"

"We didn't have anywhere to leave them. I thought I could use them to repay you. You can keep them," I said.

He glanced at them again, "That'll do. I can take them below deck."

Cody handed him the reins and he led them away. He obviously had some sort of authority on the ship. He went from one place to another, telling everyone what to do. Cody was fascinated by the sailors and watched their every move.

After another hour, the anchor was pulled up and the sails let out.

The ship lurched with the wind and started slowly down the river that would lead us to the ocean. I liked the movement. It reminded me of sitting high up in a tree on a swaying limb.

Cody and I stood at the rail, looking back at Sacramento. We had come so far to get to that place, and now we were leaving it forever. I didn't want to go, but I had to. If I couldn't be with Will, I would be with my sister.

The young man came up and leaned on the railing beside me.

I straightened; so did he. He looked at Clara sleeping against me, "What's your little lady's name?"

"Clara," I answered, studying his face.

Cody introduced himself, "I'm Cody Duckson."

He shook Cody's hand, "Nice to meet you, young man."

He looked back to me, "What's your name?"

"It's Lilly."

He nodded, "It's a pleasure to meet you, Lilly Duckson."

Without thinking I said, "Not Duckson, just Lilly," then wished I hadn't. He didn't need to know anything about me. I was relieved when Cody didn't go into my story like he had with Will.

The man smiled, "Lilly then; I'm Martin Bowdel, Captain of 'The Noble'."

"Thank you for your help, Captain Bowdel." I took the blanket we'd found on us that morning from Cody, and held it out to him, "And thank you for this."

"Keep it," He looked over the rail to the land.

I looked too. All of the sudden, looking out of a clouded window at the base of a large red-brick building, I imagined Will's face, sick and pale, watching us go.

I felt the blood drain from my face and straightened quickly. I blinked and the face was gone. Tears filled my eyes and ran down my cheeks.

Captain Bowdel saw it, "Why are you leaving California?"

"I have somewhere else to be," I answered.

June

An entire month passed without any letter from St. Louis. Margret was still quiet. I believed she had begun to see a future with Elias, but any chance at that future seemed to be fading.

I was heading out on the snowy road to take Elias's lunch to the jail when Margret ran up beside me, "I'm going with you today," she stated, "I can carry Miriam."

She took Miriam from me and set her eyes straight ahead.

Miriam was the only one who spoke on the way to the jail, babbling and smiling. I usually couldn't help but laugh when she went on like that, but I didn't feel like I could that morning. She quieted as we stepped through the door, out of the cold and into the heat of the jailhouse.

Margret gave Miriam to me as Elias noticed us and sat up on his cot. I tried to fade into the background by sitting in the chair behind Jacob's desk. He must have been out patrolling.

Margret crossed the room to stand outside the iron bars of Elias's cell. He watched her from the cot, his dark eyes as steady as ever.

He came and stood in front of her, "How are you, Margret?"

"I've been better," she answered carefully.

"I've missed you." Elias took another step forward and wrapped his hand around an iron bar. His eyebrows drew together slightly, "Do you want an explanation?"

She shook her head slowly, "Haven't I already heard it?"

"I thought you might also like to hear what I've done, what I've had to do," he paused, "what I haven't done that you're afraid I have."

Her back stiffened even more, "I guess you can tell me."

"Would you like to get a chair?"

Margret brought a chair up to the iron bars and Elias brought a chair to the other side. They sat across from each other as he started his story.

"I was assigned by the county to do an undercover job. There were conmen that had organized themselves into a group working out of a certain establishment in St. Louis." Elias leaned one elbow on a knee, just like Jacob did when he was involved in something he was telling me about work.

"I went completely undercover, staying in a hotel, saying I was an out-of-towner. When I had uncovered the ring, and arrested every man involved, I quit my job. I wanted to do something different. I wanted to do something that would allow me to settle down and be present for my family when the time came."

He sighed and his shoulders lowered, "I had to do a lot of things to keep my cover."

He paused.

"Do you want to tell me?" Margret's tone had softened considerably.

Suddenly, I was afraid of the trust he elicited. If he was a con man, he knew how to trick people!

"I would like you to know." His voice was soft, "I had to gamble. I did it all the time, in order to get into the group. I lied and stole sometimes. I had to go along with what they were doing. They were filthy, evil men."

I thought I saw tears in his dark eyes, even from across the room.

"I was involved in kidnapping a girl. I protected her while keeping my cover so that I could stop them from doing that to anyone else."

He paused and seemed to be studying Margret's face. Tears rolled down her cheeks.

Elias continued, "I know what you've been through with Lilly." He shook his head, "I don't want to bring back any of those feelings by telling you this, but I was able to prevent other families from hurting the way you have."

Margret stood a moment later and folded her arms in front of her, "I'll see you tomorrow." She turned away from the cell but looked back, "I believe you, Elias. I'll be waiting for that letter to come from St. Louis." The corners of her mouth raised slightly in a smile, "I look forward to sliding on the ice with you again."

Elias smiled back at her, "I thought you said I shouldn't be on the ice."

Margret shrugged, "We'll see."

The next day, Jacob brought the long-awaited letter to the house. He handed it to Margret, "You can open it."

She stared down at the letter and rubbed her thumb along the edge, then looked back up at Jacob, "Can we take it to the jail?"

"Sure," he nodded, "Let's take it down there now."

I turned quickly to Joshua, "Can you and Meg take care of Miriam. I'm going with them."

He nodded, "I can do that." He looked at Margret, "Be prepared Margret. It might not be what you want it to be."

Her lips tightened, and she looked down at the letter in her hands, "I'll be fine. I think I know him." She smiled over at him, "Thank you, Joshua."

Jacob and I matched Margret's hurried footsteps into town.

Elias came quickly over to the bars of his cell when we walked in, and he saw the letter in Margret's hands.

She stood close to the bars. Her hands trembled as she opened the envelope and her eyes scanned the paper.

I stood behind her with Jacob's arm around me. I couldn't see over her shoulder, but Jacob glanced at the letter, and looked down at me with a smile.

Margret looked up at Elias, and started putting the letter back into the envelope, "Well, it looks like you're an honest man, Elias Smothers."

Jacob put his hand on her back and hurried to unlock the cell door.

Margret skipped into Elias's arms, "I already believed you."

Elias smiled down at her, "I know!" He laughed, "But I'm glad there isn't any more doubt."

"Me too!"

Elias walked home with us and we invited him to stay for supper.

After we had eaten, he and Margret went for a walk. I was thankful that was settled.

Lilly

The ship was quiet most of the time. Besides the three of us, there were only sailors aboard. The sea was calm and the temperatures pleasant. Cody grew close to the captain, but not as close as he had to Will. Martin taught him about everything on the ship. At night, he sat with us and taught us about the stars.

He looked at me a lot like Will had. I wasn't sure I trusted him.

I guessed he was safe enough for Cody, but I didn't like how he thought it was funny when I felt insecure. He was the most commanding person I'd ever met. Sometimes I would imagine myself as a small bug on the ship's deck, unable to move out of the way before his heavy boot crushed me. Everyone on deck was at his mercy. He must have thought the entire world was.

If he wanted to be part of our family, I couldn't stop it, no matter how much I wanted to. He was always there when I looked up, in command and in control.

I came to avoid his gaze, his voice, his presence. I knew he didn't like it, which made me want to do it even more.

In three months, we passed by the Andes

and the bleak shores of the Atacama Desert, rounded Cape Horn in South America, and turned north there. We made an occasional stop at a port along the way but never for more than a day.

June

"Can you hand me that shovel, Meg?"

She handed it to me with a smile, "These wildflowers will look beautiful in this spot!"

I scooped up a bunch of flowers with a ball of dirt covering the roots, "Yes, I think they will."

I placed the bunch in the ground and packed the dirt around it.

"Hello, lovely gardeners!" I heard Margret calling from the road.

I straightened and Meg and I turned to see her and Elias race hand-in-hand into the yard.

"Good morning, Elias!" I smiled, "You two really do walk more than anyone I ever saw!"

"Where are Jacob and Joshua?" Margret asked.

Her eyes were sparkling and her step was light, "They're inside." I pointed to the house, "Did you want something?"

"I just want everyone out here." Her smile reached further across her face. She ran to the door and called to the boys.

They came out with Jacob holding Miriam. Margret skipped back to Elias.

He took her hand in both of his, "We wanted to tell you all we're going to get married!"

My mouth opened, but I couldn't say anything. I hugged her, even with my dirt-covered hands, "It's been coming for a long time," I said over her shoulder.

I turned quickly to Jacob standing behind me. He looked satisfied, "Jacob Plyer! You knew!"

"Elias asked me two days ago," he laughed, "I was wondering when he was going to get around to asking her!"

I turned back to Margret. She was smiling up at Elias.

Lilly

Clara's birthday was on April sixth, the day after rounding the horn. She was two years old. It was hard to imagine how far she'd come in her short life; across plains and mountains and oceans. I had come just as far. So much joy and sadness had come from the Miller's revenge on Jacob. And after all that, I was going to end in the place I began.

That night, the ship's log master died of a heart attack and was buried at sea. He was an older man and the only one on the ship, besides the Captain, who knew how to write.

Martin mourned the loss as he sat with us looking at the stars the next evening, "I depended on him. I'm busy from sunup to sundown, I don't have time to do his job as well as my own," he whined.

I continued to look at the sky. He seemed to have enough time. He spent enough hours with us each day to do ten men's jobs.

Cody was interested in the workings of the ship, as usual, "What was his job?" he asked.

"He wrote what I dictated to him," Martin answered carelessly. "He was the only man on my crew who could write. I won't find anyone out here who can write."

"Lilly can write!" Cody blurted.

Martin turned to me quickly, "You can? Of course you can!"

"No! I just learned a little. I'm not at all good at it."

Cody grinned, "Will said she had the best penmanship in the west, and that she's the fastest learner he'd ever met in his life."

I could have screamed. I didn't want to be stuck helping Martin for the rest of the trip.

Martin and I both stared at Cody, "He said that?" I asked. Cody nodded.

Will never told me. I wished I could see him again, read with him, have him back. Martin stood quickly, grabbed my arm, and pulled me toward his cabin. Cody followed close behind with little Clara holding his hand.

He sat me down at his desk in front of a piece of paper, "Write what I say."

My hand tightened around the quill. I watched with clenched teeth as Martin walked back and forth across the room.

He started speaking at an even and relaxed pace. I wrote everything he said, my shoulders relaxing as my hand formed the letters. When he finished, he bent over my shoulder to look at the paper. I nearly forgot him standing behind me as I admired the neat penmanship. I hadn't written in weeks, but the letters appeared easily on the page.

Suddenly, Martin's heavy hands were on

my shoulders, "You're wonderful, Lilly! You will be my new log master."

I cringed beneath his touch. I didn't want to be with him any more. I didn't want to write for him; but Martin said I would, so I knew I would.

My work began the next morning. Martin had me follow him all day long. He talked more than any man ought to, and he was still there when the day was finally over. He sat with us and told Cody about navigation and the stars. His voice seemed to drone on for hours. He may have looked like Will from behind, but he acted nothing like him.

When I finally lay down to go to sleep, I realized how tight my muscles had grown that day. I took a long breath. The next several weeks passed slowly as I followed him around each day scribbling endlessly.

Then one sunny day, the call rang out, "Land! Land, ho!"

June

Margret and Elias's wedding was beautiful. It was held in our front yard, and friends and neighbors stayed after to celebrate.

That evening, when everyone had gone home, Margret and Elias started down the road to Elias's house. I would miss having Margret living with us, but she wouldn't be far.

Lilly

I was with Martin when the land was spotted, paper and pen in hand, taking note of the weather and position of the sun. Cody and Clara were somewhere toward the front of the ship. As soon as I heard the cry I shoved the paper at Martin and ran to them.

Cody was holding Clara, letting her look out over the waves. I wrapped my arms around them and we scanned the horizon together. A hazy shadow of blue separated the sea from the sky. My heart swelled with the waves, and the feeling filled my entire body.

Martin let me stay with Cody and Clara the rest of that day. The next morning, the land we'd seen the day before had parted, and we sailed between the two islands. Other ships and many fishing boats sailed in every direction. Martin had a lot for me to do; he was everywhere at once.

The docks were on the island to the east. When we came near it, Martin turned to me, "Write down every word I say from here until we drop anchor. I keep a careful record of how I dock at each port."

We stood at the prow of the ship. He started shouting orders, with an occasional look back at the sails, as we came alongside the pier and dropped our anchor. I wrote down one order after another. I didn't understand what most of it meant, or how to spell it, but I did my best.

Since it wasn't a passenger ship, the deboarding was short, and I soon stood on the dock next to Cody, holding Clara on my hip.

Martin came running through the crowd. He smiled at me, "I'll have to tie up a few things, but I want to see you afterwards." He smiled one last time, and turned away without waiting for a reply.

Cody looked confused, "Did he even ask you to wait?"

I looked at Martin's retreating figure, "No, Cody."

I thought of Will. Will would have asked if we could talk later. He would have asked when I might have a few minutes and we would have agreed on a time, but not this man. If he thought I was going to wait for some unknown conversation, he was wrong. I looked back to Cody, "I don't care to wait and hear what Mr. Bowdel has to say." Then I laughed, "Let's go home!"

I took his hand and we turned away from the harbor.

Rows of buildings stood in front of us. People walked in every direction and filled the paved streets. I took a deep breath and headed for the first shop I saw. We spent the entire morning searching for a place that would sell us a handcart. The shopkeepers only laughed.

I learned we were on a sort of island, only connected to anything by its northernmost end. Anyone wanting to go west of New York City took a ferry across the Hudson River. We went directly to the ferry docks and sat down, completely exhausted.

We watched ships sailing in the river while we waited. It was over an hour before the ferry pulled into the docks and the passengers de-boarded. Almost before the previous load was out of the way, passengers started boarding for the return trip.

Cody stayed close and I held Clara as we were swept along with the crowd.

Suddenly, someone grabbed my arm, and I looked up into the face of Martin Bowdel. He pulled us to the edge of the crowd.

"What were you thinking, Lilly? Were you just going to leave?"

I walked along with the others going toward the ferry. I tried not to look at his face, "Yes, I'm leaving. I didn't come to stop here."

He walked alongside us, "But, you . . ." He was frustrated, "You didn't ask me!"

"Why would I ask you?" I said bluntly.

His face reddened, "But . . . but . . ."

He grabbed my arm and we stopped, "Lilly, I love you." His eyes looked into mine, and his grasp on my arm was firm, "Marry me."

He wasn't asking; he was ordering, just like on the ship. He was telling me to marry him. I had been afraid of that moment. Afraid that if he asked and I said no, it would happen anyway. I was afraid someday I would turn around and be Mrs. Martin Bowdel.

I stared straight up into his dark eyes, "No, Martin. I won't marry you."

"But . . ." He stopped and his grip loosened. I didn't care what he was going to say. I pulled away and ran along with the crowd and onto the ferry.

The gate closed, and we stood at the railing looking back at the dock. It was nearly desolate. Among the lingerers stood an arrogant Captain. I wondered if it was the first time he had been told no. After another moment, he turned and strutted down the street.

I looked down at Clara, glad to be rid of Martin Bowdel. Her pudgy little finger was pointing at a boat coming alongside us. It was a small fishing boat with large, linen-white sails. "Boat," she said.

I laughed and rested my cheek on her soft head, "Yes, that's right!"

When we reached the other side of the river we used the last of our money to buy food, water, and a pack for Cody to carry it all in. I tied Clara to me with a sigh, and we started west again.

June

"Um, June . . ."

I turned to Meg, who had just stepped into the kitchen, "Yes?"

Her nose crinkled, "There are two men here. They say they know Lilly!"

My heart jumped into my throat, "Lilly!"

I ran into the front room, pushing Meg in with me.

A very tall young man stood in the middle of the living room. His clothes were old, and well worn. He had dark hair and even darker eyes. He looked a little startled when he saw me.

My attention quickly turned to the man standing nearer the door. My mouth opened, "Judge Harris?"

He quickly crossed the room and hugged me! He pulled away laughing, tears streaming down his face, "I found Lilly!"

"What? Lilly?" I looked past him, searching for her, hoping she would be there, be home, alive and well. I looked back at the judge, "Where is she? Tell me! Is she---"

"She's alive, June! She's alive." His hands were resting on my shoulders.

I started to tremble, "Where is she?"

"She's coming. I found her sick on the trail to California. The Millers were taking her to Sacramento with them, to search for gold."

"You came without her? Where is she?"

"She was too sick to bring back, and I went to another wagon train while I was waiting for her to get strong again. I got sick while I was there, and I lost track of her. I went on to Sutter's Mill myself and found this fellow."

He moved aside so I could see the tall young man again. I stepped up to him and nodded, "I'm June Plyer."

"I'm Will Haskim," he said in a deep voice.

"Do you know Lilly?"

His dark eyes brightened, "I know her."

The judge smiled, "Sit down, June. We'll tell you everything."

The story was long, evoking tears, anger, smiles, and laughter. They told me about Lilly's journey with Cody, and finding Clara and Will.

Judge Harris and Will had traveled five months to get back, going east while every other traveler headed west.

Judge Harris found Will at Cody's aunt and uncle's home. Will had just returned from Sacramento after recovering from Cholera, to find Lilly, Cody, and Cora all gone.

"I was lucky the Judge found me," Will said. "I didn't know how I was going to get to Lilly."

Judge Harris put his hand firmly on Will's sturdy shoulder, "I couldn't have asked for a better traveling companion. He's a good man."

I studied Will's smile, his broad shoulders and strong hands. I looked back up to his face. I wanted to know him better. "And how does Lilly feel about you?"

He looked down, smiled a little, and cleared his throat. But then he looked back up at me, "I've been part of Lilly's life, her family really, for a year and a half. She's cared for the children, cared for me. She's amazing, June." His smile widened, "I love her. And I'm going to ask her to marry me when she gets here."

Lilly

We walked through forests and hills for six weeks.

When we started getting higher up into the mountains, I knew it wouldn't be long before we would be home with Jacob and June. But first, I found myself walking along a path toward a home I had known long before.

We came to a clearing in the trees, the afternoon sunshine lighting the tiny cottage that stood at the center.

I stopped.

June

I grew to love Will very quickly. It seemed like the whole town knew him soon after he arrived. Of course, everyone wanted to meet him and hear about Lilly, what she had been through, and the things she had done.

Will told them stories, always showing us a side of Lilly we hadn't seen when she was here.

Sometimes I worried I wouldn't know her when she got back. But then I'd watch Will; she had apparently fallen in love with him. Getting to know him made me feel like I was getting to know her too.

Lilly

Thoughts and feelings rushed over me. It seemed like no time had passed since I had lived in that cottage with its deteriorating thatch, sun-bleached walls, and creaking wood porch. I hadn't known anything about the people or places, or the love that lay beyond that circle of trees.

No matter how Aunt Matilda and I cared and watched out for each other, I saw then that I had never loved or been loved. We worked and ate and talked together, and that was all.

I had a family now. They were mine, and I was theirs. Aunt Matilda had been satisfied and preferred our existence in that place. She decided to live her life without family and love, but I wouldn't. I wanted to be with Will so much in that moment.

June

"I'm going to get you!" Will said, chasing Miriam around our small front room.

She squealed as she hobbled away from him, only for him to scoop her up and lift her above his head.

I laughed, "Watch out! She'll be stronger than you some day when you're an old man, and she'll get you back."

"I'll make it up to her by then." He lowered her to kiss her small cheek, "Won't I, Miriam? You'll just love your Uncle Will!"

A laugh burst from Jacob who had been sitting in the corner reading, "You sure she'll want to marry you?"

Will set Miriam back down on the floor, "I'm hoping."

Lilly

Cody stood beside me, watching my face as I thought, "Is this home?"

I looked at the cottage again and shook my head, "No, not anymore."

We walked on past the cottage and into the woods on the opposite side of the clearing.

Just as the sun sank below the horizon, we came to a peak overlooking a village with sunlight reflecting from the rooftops.

I didn't have to wonder what families in those homes felt; I knew.

Walking through town the next evening, I didn't gape at the buildings or shrink from the people. I didn't care when passersby stared at the two weary travelers and their baby. In a few minutes, we stood in front of a small white-washed house.

I turned to Cody, "This is home."

We both stood staring at the house. Thousands of miles had made us a family and brought us there.

Sunset filled the sky with color, and lightning bugs started flickering. Clara squirmed against me, and I unwound the old apron and set her down. She looked all around her, pointing and speaking unintelligibly about all the new things she saw.

A little girl around Clara's age ran out of the front door. The two babies came close to each other, stopped in the middle of the path, and studied one another.

Then a voice came from inside the house, "Miriam!" June laughed, "Where are you going?"

June tripped out the door, started off the porch, and stopped.

She looked at the two little girls then toward the road where Cody and I stood at the edge of the yard.

Once again, I felt as though I looked into my own reflection. Her brown curls resting on her shoulders and blue eyes gazing at me were all so familiar.

I took a step toward her, "June," I whispered.

Her eyes lit up, "Lilly!"

We ran, and hugged each other tightly.

Her voice quivered, "You're here! Oh, Lilly, I missed you so much. We've been waiting!"

I pulled away and held her at arm's length, "Waiting? You still thought I'd come back!"

"We--- Oh, Lilly! She pulled me close again, but turned away suddenly, and called back to the house, "Lilly's here! She's back!"

Jacob, Joshua, and Meg ran out of the house. I hugged them all at once, "I thought I'd never see any of you again!"

The little girl came up behind me and

grabbed my skirt. I looked down and touched the top of the baby's head, "Who is this little one?"

June's eyes sparkled, "She's my little girl." She picked her up, "This is Miriam." She looked back up at me, "Miriam, this is Lilly."

I looked around at my family, "Where's Margret?" I asked.

They smiled, "She's married!" Jacob said.

"Married? When did this happen?"

"Just six weeks ago. His name is Elias. I think you'll really like him!"

"Can we see them soon?"

"Of course!" June said.

I didn't quite know what to say; but looking around at their smiling faces, I remembered what June had said.

I turned to her, "You've been waiting for me?"

"Will's been here!" Meg blurted.

I spun around to Cody, "Will!" I knelt to pick up Cora, "He's alive!" I turned Jacob, "Where is he? Is he here?"

"He's staying in Margret and Elias's barn while he builds a house."

"Can we go there now? Where do they live?"

June

Lilly looked frantic, "Yes, let's go," I said.

I picked up Miriam and we started walking down the road to Margret and Elias's house.

My heart beat in my throat. I walked next to Lilly. She looked a little older, and she was holding her own adopted baby on her hip, with an adopted son walking beside her.

She had been through so many things, and done so much. She had spent time with our parents, Cody's parents, his aunt and uncle, and fallen in love with Will.

Lilly

June had been studying me and Cody and Clara. I felt like she should feel unfamiliar, but she didn't. She was still June; my sister and my friend.

We went around a small curve in the road, and there ahead of us Margret was walking with her husband. I couldn't believe she was married!

I started running toward her, "Margret!" Clara bounced on my hip as I ran, "Margret, it's me!"

The couple paused in their walk, then she broke away, ran to meet me, and threw her arms around me, "Lilly! Oh, Lilly!"

She smelled like flowers and fresh air, "I missed you so much!" I said into her thick hair.

I pulled away from her and glanced at Elias coming up behind her smiling.

"You got married!"

She smiled, "I did!" She reached back and grabbed Elias's hand to bring him forward, "This is Elias."

"It's nice to meet you, Elias."

"You too, Lilly! We've been waiting for you."

I laughed, "I guess everyone has!"

My hands were shaking. I was so close to

seeing Will! "Where's Will? Is he here?"

Both of their smiles widened, "He's been gone for the afternoon. He'll be back soon, I'm sure," Margret said, her eyes sparkling.

June

We finally caught up with Lilly.

"Do you know where he went?" She was asking.

I was becoming just as anxious as Lilly was, "Is he out?" I asked Margret.

"I'm sure he'll be home soon!"

She glanced back at the house, "Why don't we all go inside?"

Lilly looked impatient but smiled, "That would be fine." She gave Cody's hand a short squeeze, "It won't be long now."

She adjusted Clara on her hip and started after Margret and Elias toward the house.

Lilly

I felt my heart pounding every moment, waiting to hear Will's voice.

I couldn't sit still. I left the living room and went out to the front porch.

It was getting late in the evening but it wasn't dark yet, and the trees were soft in the light. I leaned against a wooden beam supporting the porch roof and looked up at the sky.

I could hear Cody laughing and Clara babbling with Jacob and June's little Miriam. Having Will there would make my family complete.

I heard the door open behind me and Margret came out onto the porch. She was gazing up at the stars, just beginning to show in the sky, "They're beautiful, aren't they?"

"Yes, they are."

"You really love Will, don't you?"

I nodded, and smiled at her, "He makes me feel more special than anyone I've ever met, and he's more special," I whispered.

She wrapped her arms around me and I let myself cry. She held me while the tears I had saved for months fell onto her shoulder.

We pulled away from each other and I

smiled. I had thought Will was dead, but suddenly he was alive!

"Are you alright?" Margret asked, wiping away her own tears.

I laughed, "Of course! He's here!"

We started laughing and the sound rang through the trees.

June

I stepped out onto the porch, and into a ripple of laughter, "Are you two having fun?"

They turned their happy faces to me. I couldn't help laughing too, and hugging Lilly close to me again.

She stepped away, "I missed my sister," she said.

"I missed my sister too. But, we're together now!" I looked into her eyes, "All of us!" I laughed again. "I couldn't be happier."

Lilly

We turned back to the stars. The sky was still a pale blue. It reminded me of evenings on the trail.

So many nights, I lay in our wagon with the wind blowing, or the snow falling. I hadn't imagined bringing Clara and Cody back to this place.

And now Will.

I thought of our conversation the last night we'd been together; the night we walked into town and heard about the fire in Sacramento.

He had asked me about courting! I wondered if he felt the same after all this time.

I had tried to detach my feelings from the memories I had of him when I thought he was gone, and now all those feelings had come flooding back.

I smiled at the way he laughed when I had asked what a squash was, the way his eyes lit up when he found something to teach me, the way he lifted Clara over his head to make her giggle.

June

My eyes traveled from Lilly's smile to the road in front of the house.

I grabbed her arm, and pointed, "It's Will!"

Lilly

I looked quickly toward the road. A tall figure was walking down the road in the waning light. My throat tightened, and I tripped off the porch and ran to him.

We threw our arms around each other, "Will!" I sobbed into his shoulder. I couldn't stop the tears, "You're here! I felt like it wasn't real when they told me you were alive!" I looked up at him, "Will, I love you."

He wiped my tears away with strong, calloused fingers and brushed a stray curl from my face. "I love you too!" he laughed and brought me close to him again.

After a moment, he pushed me away but kept his hands on my waist, "We made it."

"We did," I giggled.

His eyes sparkled as he studied my face with a playful smirk, "Before your ship left Sacramento, Martin Bowdel told everyone he was going to marry you. It's still just Lilly isn't it, not Lilly Bowdel?"

"You know me, Will." I smiled, "I'm always just Lilly."

His eyes were dancing, "Not for long."

I wrapped my arms around his neck, "Lilly

Haskim. I like the sound of that."

He laughed, "Let's go tell the kids."

We turned back to the house and were met by Cody running to the road carrying Clara. Will hugged Cody close and let him sob into his shoulder while he held Clara in the other arm.

June

Will hugged the children for a long time before they all dropped to their knees and huddled together.

They cried and smiled. They embraced and touched each other's faces, and embraced again.

Cody let himself cry hard on Will's shoulder. Clara was only smiling and poking Will's face with her soft little fingers.

Lilly

When we were able to compose ourselves, we stumbled back into Margret and Elias's house.

I smiled for days.

On Saturday, we made our way to the church for the wedding; Jacob and June, Margret and Elias, Joshua, Meg, Miriam, Cody and Clara, and Will and me.

Judge Harris stood on the front steps of the church. I ran to him and hugged him.

He held me tightly, "I'm sorry I couldn't get back to you."

I pulled away and shook my head, "If you had, I wouldn't have found Will."

Will put his arm around me and laughed, "Don't be sorry, Judge. I'm not!"

"I can see that," he smiled and ushered us all into the chapel.

Everyone took their seats, and Will and I stood in front of the Judge and joined hands.

I looked up at Will; at his dark eyes and steady smile. I would be happy all of my life with him.

The Judge looked happier than I'd ever seen him, "We've come together this day to join this man and this woman in holy matrimony."

June

The judge looked to Will, "You may say your vows now."

Will turned his full attention to Lilly, "Lilly, I take you to be my wife, to have and to hold, to love, from this day forward, for better, for worse, for richer, for poorer, in sickness and in health, to love and to cherish always."

Lilly looked back into his eyes, "Will, I take you to be my husband, to have and to hold, to love, from this day forward. I have seen your devotion and love, and I place my trust in you, and my heart with you always."

They smiled at each other for a moment and turned back to the judge.

Lilly

The judge smiled, "Will, you may now kiss your bride."

I looked up at Will, his dark eyes sparkling, "I couldn't love you more, Lilly," he whispered as he bent down to kiss me.

Historical Note

I had no idea of the journey Lilly would take me on when I started writing this book.

This tale begins, roughly around Knoxville, Tennessee.

The town Jacob and June live in is a general reflection of the size and type of town Knoxville was in 1850. It is not a specific, real-life town.

The trial held against the Millers is most likely technically flawed in many ways. I couldn't find much information about the laws and procedures of how a trial worked at that time.

Lilly and the Millers starting west was a surprise to me. Even after their journey began, I was convinced they would be apprehended before making it very far.

The Rocky Mountain spotted fever was not actually spread from one person to another, though they believed it was. Rather, it is a bacterial infection spread by tick bites. Most of the symptoms Lilly experienced are true to life. The full explanation, and the realities would be rather gruesome to explain in detail in the story. It is characterized by a high fever, muscle aches, nausea, etc. The illness also involved confusion and neurological changes; this is displayed in Lilly's feverish state. Many wagon trains were afflicted with the Rocky Mountain spotted fever.

The travelers most likely believed the illness was contagious as a result of the large numbers of people in the same train that contracted it. This came from being in an area where the ticks were infected with the disease.

Many wagon trains started their journey in the winter of 1849, as the country caught wind of the gold found at Sutter's Mill in Coloma, California. Greed took many of these people west; people like the Millers. Others were drawn to the place for its booming commerce, as were Will's mother and father and the Ducksons.

The route they went by would have typically taken about two hundred days to travel, but was lengthened by the illness they suffered.

A lot of time was invested in the research of the Forty-Mile Desert crossing, seeking for accuracy in an experience so foreign to my own. Pioneers did cross the desert on foot in order to spare the oxen pulling their wagons. The best hours for travel were at night when temperatures were lower, which helped in conserving water.

Along the last stretch of the Forty-Mile Desert crossing, travelers often passed the carcasses of oxen and possessions left by those who had gone before. Finding Will and his father and sister was an example of the despair that was strewn all along that desert.

The crossing of the Forty-Mile Desert in this story was dangerously late, placing them at the base of the Sierra Nevada mountains at a time of year when they would face freezing temperatures and heavy snowfall at the higher elevations.

Crossing the Sierra Nevada mountains was done fairly quickly in this story, and I only briefly addressed the hardships faced. In this same place and time of year, the Donner Party met their doom, three years before.

The fire that allowed Will to find work in Sacramento was in April 1850. Eight city blocks were destroyed in that fire.

In October 1850, a riverboat called "New World" sailed up the Sacramento river and brought news of California's admittance into the Union, as well as the cholera epidemic. Nearly eighty percent of the population either came down with the illness or left the city.

Will's illness was only slightly extended for the sake of the story. Individuals who did die of Cholera at the time, would do so within several days of when their symptoms appeared, as a result of dehydration. Will would have been quite weak for some time while recovering from the disease; therefore, it is conceivable that he would not yet have returned to Frank and Harriet's and would still be resting and recovering somewhere in the city.

While the boats traveling back east from California would not generally carry passengers, Lilly traveled on a boat going back to New York City. Some aspects of this voyage are unrealistic.

Groundwork laid for constructing the Panama Canal had just begun in 1850, and would not be completed until August 15th 1914. Gold-seekers did go west by way of ship; sailing from New York to the eastern shore of Panama, taking eighteen days to cross the isthmus. They would make their way to Panama's western shore, where they would board a second ship. Those ships took them north to California.

I decided taking Lilly through the Panama jungle would quite honestly be a little crazy. Ships did return to New York from California in order to board more passengers bound for gold-country. This journey took four to five and a half months, going around Cape Horn in South America.

Will and Judge Harris were able to make the trip across the United Stated on foot in five months. That would mean they walked about twenty miles a day, having them arrive about two months before Lilly, Cody, and Clara, who traveled by boat for about five months and walked for about six weeks.

Many months of research were put into this story to give it the right feel and historical accuracy. As a writer, I took liberties in manipulating certain facts; but I tried to use as much of the truth as possible while keeping the story interesting.

Every character, and the events in this book are a product of my imagination. Any similarity to actual people and events is purely coincidental.

I am not a historian. I read and researched, but I'm positive there are many mistakes.

History shows us how similar humans are and always have been. I spent time over the months reading first person accounts, and enjoyed the journals of many different individuals. Each described the same events from their own perspective, yet many feelings remained consistent.

Made in the USA
Coppell, TX
21 September 2021